HOLLYWOOD ASS.

Jonas Eriksson

AUTHOR'S NOTE

Most of the names, events and places in this book are fictional and I have taken some creative liberties with the rest. All errors or inconsistencies are my own fault. I want to thank my editor and love, Lenah Caruana, for reading and editing the manuscript and my friend and top class designer, Etienne Bugeja, for creating the cover. /JE.

HOLLYWOOD ASS.

Dedication

To *B*.
You're the best.
Thanks for helping me tell the tale.

/Darryl.

***

Introduction

It took me quite a while to make up my mind on whether I was going to write this book or not. I knew I had a story to tell, that it was something out of the ordinary and thanks to diligent diary-keeping during the time it happened, I had the material. But then I had other things to take into consideration: could I mention real names? Would I be able to do the story justice? Would *B*, the famous actress I had worked for and the main character in this book, give her consent?

There were loads of question marks, but in the end I only needed one answer and it was *B*'s encouragement to get the story told. She said she preferred it from getting a half-assed biography written by some ghostwriter who didn't know her and she liked that it was more about our friendship than her fame. It was a gutsy move on her part, because this story tells you about the most trying time in her life, a time where she hit rock bottom in her personal life, made a fool out of herself in front of millions of viewers and fans and experienced a close shave with death. I can't express enough how thankful I am to her for not only allowing me, but also helping me, tell it.

Because it is in many ways *our* story. And I have tried to treat it with the respect it deserves by not mentioning real names. I think it would make it more about their fame and the careers, and not the lives and events around them.

I wrote this book not only because I think it's an interesting tale about people's struggle with fame and relationships, but also because it has something to say about life and how unpredictable and magical it can be. It's a story I hope my future kids will read to get to know me better, because I think it teaches them exactly what my parents taught me, that everything is possible and your dreams are always within reach, if you just act through your heart and not only your mind.

Ultimately, I see this book as a tribute to friendship.

Thanks for reading.

Darryl Glendale,
New York.

***

It's hard not to be captivated by red carpet events and their flashing lights and ridiculously beautiful people milling about smiling like this was the night of their lives and they were oh-so-happy to see this person and that person and spit out countless stale-sounding comments like "you look amazing", "you were terrific in that role" and "have you lost weight?" followed by a sincere look, secretly saying, *I'm an actor, I'm really good at faking things.*

You see my point. You're simply spellbound by these "fame orgies" until you've been to like 30 of them. Then you're just robotic and going through the motions. Okay, okay, I might just as well come out and say the *real* reason why I wasn't so ecstatic about the flamenco-colored rug experience with extra everything - it's because I was just an onlooker, an extra among the blessed few who got the chance to dazzle the world with their looks, skills and ad-libbed one-liners. I wasn't an actor, I was an assistant. I was maybe the best damn assistant out there, but in that glamorous part of the world, it didn't count for a whole lot.

When you're a celebrity assistant your performance actually only counts with one person in the world and that's your employer. I was lucky in that respect, because *B* was always appreciative of me and what I did for her, something which made me work extra hard and really appreciate her. That's also a strong reason we became friends - mutual respect.

But *B* sometimes had a hard time to respect herself and her career. She was an immensely successful romantic comedy actress and the star of movies that made women all over the world go *"oooh"* and guys go *"uuuugh"*. You know the kind. I'm not saying they're *bad* movies and I understood the charm in *B*'s performances, but neither *B* nor I were into films where you could predict the whole story line just by reading the DVD cover blurb. That's one reason she didn't really respect herself.

And that was in part what lead to the famous red carpet disaster. And I'm not using the D-word lightly here like some people do when they spilled coffee on a pair of pants or are ten minutes late for a school play. What I'm talking about kept Hollywood buzzing with excitement and bewilderment for months. Was it a bit exaggerated? Yes, but everything in Hollywood is exaggerated and when Miss Perfect, which was the character she played in almost all of her movies, threw up in front of millions of TV-viewers and a whole bunch of other celebrities, the media spin machine went into overdrive.

When *B* had launched her projectile vomit, right there on the red carpet, the world stopped for a second and stared at the mash of white wine, shrimp, guacamole and God knows what else, and asked the obvious question: *What the hell happened?* The famous TV-presenter, who witnessed the whole thing from only a meter away and probably got some of her regurgitated food on his shoes, probably asked the same thing. He was frozen and pale, a rare look on his always polished and controlled facade. Luckily, her husband and colleague, which we for simplicity's sake call *A*, acted fast and pulled her away from the action and the crowds and into the bathroom where the vomiting continued for a few minutes, until her stomach was empty and I wanted to throw up just because of the rancid smell filling the room.

A didn't look very happy when we, 15 minutes later, escorted her from the scene of the crime and through a horde of paparazzi to our black Range Rover parked just outside the venue. Driver Don was waiting for us and I remember marveling at how calm he looked. But then again, Don had muscle pains and a subscription for medical marijuana to deal with that pain, so he was probably just high.

"This is it." *A* fumed in the car, "This is the last fucking time you embarrass me. I'm sick of your tantrums and you behaving like a lost teenager when we should really have a stable marriage with children and a life to be proud of. I've had it."

I glanced over at Don, who drove casually and didn't seem to be bothered by the verbal explosion taking place in the back of the car. More benefits of being high, I guess. Me, I was very uncomfortable.

"Fuck you, I didn't embarrass anyone. I'm sick and told you we shouldn't have come," *B* has been voted one of the most beautiful women in the world by several magazines, but here she looked more like a zombie and she still had a dash of vomit at the side of her mouth. I remember feeling extremely sorry for her then, something I had done for a few months already, because of her constant mood-changes, her excessive drinking and lingering depression.

A wasn't one to step away from a fight and continued, "You're not sick, you're sideways. I saw how you prepared for this evening, Martini after Martini. You wanted to make a scene, didn't you? You want our life to collapse."

"Shut up!" *B* said, while leaning her heavy head against the window. She didn't have much of an answer to *A*, because in a way, we all knew he was right. Her drinking had been out of control for a while and now she had finally reached rock bottom with a slam.

After driving for little more than half-an-hour we got home to the couple's sprawling white, multi-million dollar mansion in the Hollywood Hills and while the couple quickly escaped to their quarters, I sat down with a beer in the kitchen and wrote in my diary. I was simply too afraid to go online to face the storm and the six missed calls from agent Julianne I just couldn't care less about.

All I could feel was how my heart bled for *B*. I knew that somehow the negative trend in her life had to be reversed, but I didn't have a clue on how to do it and felt helpless thinking about it.

B, on the other hand, had her ideas.

***

Before I go into what happened *after* the vomit incident that launched it all, I think it makes sense to tell you *how* I became a celebrity assistant to an A-list actress (if you hate back-story, you can skip this section). As you might know or guess, there's no Hollywood unemployment office or any other shortcut to the wealthy and famous, because like everything in show business, it's about contacts and catching a break. Luckily for me, I knew Rob, a slick bastard with a fast mouth and the ability to sell sand in the Sahara. Rob didn't sell sand, but houses, and he helped the celebrity couple, let's call them the Johnsons, to find and negotiate their Hollywood Hills mansion. He got quite a commission for it too as you can imagine and that's why he drove a brand new Lamborghini.

I got to know Rob through my previous employment, being an assistant to the chief executive officer at a large pharmaceutical company. The CEO, a white-haired, dull and always tidy older man with an S&M magazine collection (his compensation for being more boring than spreadsheets, I suppose) in his bottom drawer, was looking for property and asked me to find the right agent and a proper selection for his perusal. I started the search engine and quickly stumbled upon an image of bleached-teeth Rob, who according to the testimonials on his websites was one of the best in the business when it came to finding lavish homes for the ridiculously rich. We met for lunch and it didn't take us long to get along, as we both shared a healthy disdain for the client (aka my boss) and when Rob said he might have an opportunity for me to get away from my job, I had to hear him out.

What he told me was that his car-loving golfing buddy, who also happened to be a Hollywood movie star, was looking for an assistant, primarily for his even more famous wife. Rob described them as the nicest couple and if I didn't mind taking my assistant life up a notch, both when it came to demands and living standards, he'd recommend me. I think I said yes before he even finished the sentence.

I met the Johnsons for coffee in a high-end LA restaurant. At first I was very nervous about meeting this superstar couple, but their rather modest and easy-going behavior relaxed me and we immediately took a liking to each other. I was instantly taken with *B* and vividly remember her wearing this green and revealing summer dress where I expected one of her breasts to jump out and every second the celebrity couple weren't looking directly at me, I watched that left boob with intent.

In the end it never came out, but a contract did - I was hired. Apparently Rob had sold them on, and here I quote, my upbeat, yet composed personality and top-notch organizational skills. He didn't have to sell me on the job though: good pay, all the perks I could dream of and working daily with one of the most beautiful women in the world. You could say I'd won the job lottery.

I remember my first day, I felt like a kid at summer camp, sleeping away from home for the first time in his life.

I drove up to the house in my slightly battered Toyota Prius and had to call a number to be let in through the massive iron gates. My heart was thumping and I was sweating profusely under my shirt and still had problems to grasp what was happening, but as soon as *A* came to greet me outside with a huge smile on his face, I felt a little bit better. He was intimidatingly handsome, but looked kind, in fact far nicer than he did in the movies I had seen him in, all of them featuring more explosions and gunfire than dialogue. He gave me a tour of the house, which was every bit as impressive as I thought it would be and introduced me to the team members working there, the team I was supposed to coordinate. Then it was time to meet *B* and start working on the day's schedule.

B was riding an exercise bike in black hot pants and a training bra when I entered the mansion gym. She turned around and said "Hi Darryl!" with a big smile on her face. She was preparing for a role with several beach scenes and her training regime was fierce. I was a bit surprised not to see a personal trainer around, but it turned out he was sick that day. You never see a celebrity in a gym without a personal trainer, trust me.

It's difficult not to be taken by *B*'s beauty. Simple, yet perfect somehow, it made me slightly weak in the knees. I hadn't had a relationship for some time and my confidence around women wasn't as good as it perhaps should've been (I'm not unattractive and quite funny) and most females sensed this well before I got the chance to even say hello, but it didn't take me long to feel comfortable around *B*, probably because I wasn't trying to date her. We just had great chemistry from the start. This was already evident on the first day when she was in a good mood thanks to a successful appearance on a popular talk show the night before. She seemed confident and in control and I remember being impressed by her from the get-go.

She was far from the dark place she would land in later.

***

They day after the "incident" started with me waking up at ten-thirty (it was my day off) and thinking for a second it was all a bad dream. It was a blissful moment, but it ended as soon I reached for the iPhone and saw all my text messages.

It was all over the place, of course, the vomit, everywhere your browser could take you. Twitter was blowing up with jokes, the Youtube clips were already in the hundreds of thousands, and the talk shows were busy writing top ten lists, all dedicated to the disaster. The comments were pretty much aligned, with some variations. Some called her a drunk (half-true), some predicted she was pregnant (not true at all), and some said she was going through a rough time in her life and that a divorce might be looming (maybe true). I knew B's agent Julianne was probably trying to spin this around to the best of her abilities, but the fact of the matter was that B had made a royal ass out of herself and for that I felt really sad. B was not only my employer, because after four years as her loyal assistant, we had also become good friends. At least as good as you could be in such a working relationship.

After showering and getting dressed, I headed down to the kitchen for my morning espresso. To my surprise I saw B out in the garden, lying in a deck chair by the pool, dressed in a lime-green bathing suit and holding some kind of drink.

"Can you get me another *Smoothme*, Fred?" I heard her shout to the pool boy and gardener, 19-year-old gay and aspiring make-up artist Fredric Thomson, who had started working there three months prior and despite the rough patch *B* had been in, really seemed to enjoy it. The star glow can be very addictive, especially if you're 19.

Fredric, who was fiddling with some plants in the small poolside garden sighed, said "sure" in a high-pitched voice and walked inside to make *B*'s favorite drink, a fruit and vegetable smoothie with a generous dose of vodka in it. This had become her way of dealing with a hangover, just smooth it over and get on with it. She was sadly starting to become quite experienced at this.

"Don't put any vodka in this one, Fred, we can't have her drunk before lunchtime," I said and switched on the espresso machine.

Beautiful dark java slipped out into my cup and I looked at my phone again, expecting Julianne to call at any minute, wanting to discuss the damage or chat to *B*. On my employers behalf, I had become a filter when it came to unwanted calls and most people knew there was no point in calling her directly, which made my phone vibrate more than a nymphomaniac's sex toy. I was okay with it and according to a test I did many years ago, I have a really high stress tolerance, a requirement for anyone working in the insane entertainment business.

I managed to just about finish my morning shot before I heard her cracked voice calling me, like a crying child begging my name. I took a deep breath and headed out to the pool.

"How are we doing today?" I said, feeling like a

caretaker in an insane asylum.

"I'm feeling great, full of energy and ready to take on the world, what do you think?" *B* said, sarcastically. We had thankfully progressed beyond the polite in our communication. Now we were more like an old married couple.

"I hear you. So...I expect Julianne to call any minute you know. You feel like taking that or?"

"I've got nothing to say to her. I know she's great at turning things around, but right now my world is pretty much painted black as you can understand. I of course knew that things weren't great, but this bad? I mean, Charlie Sheen is probably rubbing his hands somewhere."

I sat down next to her and put my hand on her shoulder, "I know it's shitty and I'm not going to give you some bullshit cliché to feel better, but I just want to say that when you've hit rock bottom there's only one way and that's up."

"You're such a fucking Teletubby sometimes, Darryl, but I still love you," she said giving me a rare smile. Not rare when judging by how she normally was, but sadly seldom those last few months.

I returned her smile and gave her some good advice: "I don't think it's such a great idea for you to lay in the sun and drink smoothie cocktails when you're hung-over. What do you say I have Jorge fix you a nice lunch and then we'll go for a drive or something? How does that sound?" Our drives and walks usually made her feel better and somewhere deep down I hoped even such a disappointing situation could be remedied by exercise and good company.

"Okay," she said, "I'll have the one Fredric is preparing and then I'll take a shower. Deal?"

"Deal. But no alcohol this time, just a regular smoothie, okay?"

"Mhmm," she mumbled like a kid refused her candy.

I went back to the kitchen to check on Fredric, who was struggling with the mixer. Fredric had green hands and knew styling and make-up like it came in his breast-milk, but couldn't tell the stove from the fridge, so I helped him by clicking on the wall-switch.

"She's really off the tracks, isn't she?" Fredric said above the mixer noise and gave me a concerned look.

"Yes, it's bad. We need to do something, but I don't know what."

"Why can't we call AA? Or a psychologist? We need an intervention!" Fredric's voice traveled up to a pitch I thought wasn't known to man, at least *a* man. I think part of him got really excited about the drama *B*'s life provided. After four years together, I wasn't excited by it, just worried.

"I don't know. We've tried to talk her into therapy, counseling, even some holistic stuff, but she's not budging. This goes deep and if she's not seeing it as a problem herself, then we can't force her to do anything."

Fredric poured the thick green mixer liquid into a glass and said, "Can we at least get her to drink some water and do a facial? If she keeps this up her skin will be hosting next months blackheads-fest."

He was right. *B*'s star glow had been hijacked by the evil Dr. Vodka and his mischievous cousin Deep Depression and we needed to guide her towards a better, brighter path. Wherever this lay.

"You know what?" I said, "Call that dermatologist lady who came last time, she was a pro and *B* was really happy with the results."

"Roger that." Fredric said, handed me the smoothie and strutted off like a flamingo bird on speed.

***

Before heading out towards Runyon Canyon, I managed a long and disturbing call with Julianne. Julianne was almost always pissed at something and after the "vomit incident" she obviously had plenty to be angry about. Besides, she didn't like me much and didn't understand what my role had become. Before, I was managing and coordinating most of the time, everything from sorting out dry-cleaning, to booking appointments, arranging schedules and plans, and now I delegated most of those things to Fredric and the rest of the team. I had my hands full just being around *B* and making sure her every wish came true. I was her one-man entourage and had strangely become her link to the rest of the world. Yes, even between her and her husband sometimes.

I put on my tracksuit and headed over to the garage to take out the Range Rover, when I stumbled upon *A*, polishing one of his many luxurious toys, the Ferrari F430 Scuderia. He looked like he had gotten dressed in a time machine in his tucked-in white t-shirt and tight, stonewashed jeans and cowboy boots. He was an attractive man with a muscular jaw and bulging biceps, but had the dress sense of someone collecting bottles for a living. This was one thing that irked *B*, but she said that, like most men, he was unchangeable in this respect. He looked up at me and I followed a bead of sweat roll down his forehead with my eyes.

16

"What's up, man?" he said. *A* sometimes talked like he was still in college. Maybe he thought this was how black guys talked, that we couldn't utter a sentence without inserting words like *man* or *dawg* or worse, the dreaded n-word. Since I had worked alongside him for years and was a book worm, he should've known better.

"I'm taking her for a walk," I said, and realized I was talking about his wife like she was a dog. If only she was as well-trained and easy to please.

"That's good. Hope it makes her feel better," *A*'s voice came out dead as timber and reflected the emotional investment he had shown for her the last year, at least according to *B*. He had a knack of retreating down to his four-wheeled friends as soon as the going got rough. And it had been rather rough lately.

"She's worried you're still angry with her." I put my hands in my tracksuit pockets and leaned against the door frame. Talking about *B* with *A* always made me feel strange, because I was *B*'s assistant, but at the same time a close friend of both. I didn't like to take sides or listen to the rants of a married couple in a desperate need of counseling.

A focused his eyes back on the Ferrari logo, the stampeding horse which was now so shiny it looked like it would spring to life and run away by itself. "Well, she can keep on worrying, because I am. She really took it to another level last night. I mean, how would you react in my shoes?"

"Pretty much the same, I guess." I said, and thought nobody knows what they would do in another person's shoes, but I didn't think *A*'s reaction was strange either. What concerned me was how much he had managed to slip away prior to the vomit. It didn't strike me like he wanted to *fight* for their marriage, but even the all-seeing assistant couldn't know everything of course. There are two sides to every story and naturally I mostly got *B*'s point of view.

He looked back up at me with his sharp blue eyes and said, "I don't know what to do anymore. She's become this other person, so deeply unhappy and strange. It's not who I fell in love with that's for sure. She refuses to seek help for it too, like she doesn't see a problem that's right in front of her, you know?" *A* was waiting for a guy response, some agreement, a feeling of camaraderie.

I couldn't shake the feeling that he was contemplating a divorce. After all it wasn't the most uncommon thing in Hollywood for people to say, "I've had it with you and your obsession with yourself, your constant traveling and your absurdly elevated need for attention," although it was a mirror image they were talking to. How could you make such a strenuous concept as marriage work in a world so demanding? There are obviously no secrets, only hard work, and my guess was that *A* had grown tired of working hard for the relationship, he wanted to see some results.

"It's very frustrating," I said, feeling uneasy about being sandwiched in between their struggles, "We're heading out now, I'll see if I can talk some sense into her."

"Good luck," *A* said without a hint of belief in his voice and returned to his Ferrari, a car that always performed flawlessly, something I'm sure he wished for in his wife.

***

Runyon Canyon is the celebrity-prone park above Los Angeles, which has featured in countless of movies and series, especially from the 80s. The fact that it's near high-end neighborhoods like the Hollywood Hills makes it possible to run into a celebrity at any time and if you were lucky you might even have stumbled upon the Johnsons taking an evening walk or a morning jog.

I parked the black Range Rover and *B* walked out in her velvety blue Juicy Couture track suit and adjusted her pants and her hair. I had told her the outfit wasn't in fashion anymore and that it made her look like a big baby in overalls, but she said she loved the material too much to let it go. And let's face it, when your new claim to fame is vomiting on one of the bigger televised awards in the calendar year, showing up in a three-year-old tracksuit is not going to do much to your reputation. I was wearing a grey t-shirt with "Who let the dogs out" in big block letters, so perhaps it wasn't the right time to be pointing out fashion mistakes.

B started walking down the so called Star trail with verve, her long legs striding and picking up speed rapidly and her head focused forwards. She was apparently eager to shed both calories and inner demons and that was a positive sign. *You go girl!* I thought to myself in my inner gay voice. Every man has an inner gay voice, at least if you spend as much time around a woman (without sleeping with her) as I did.

I jogged a few steps to catch up with her, "Aren't you an eager beaver today?" I said, trying to keep my voice upbeat. She needed me to be on my A-game today and remind her the world wasn't ending just because she had *literally* spilled her guts on TV.

"I'm no beaver, I'm Barney the drunken dinosaur. Please keep the tempo with me, I can't run into someone today. I just can't." B said, annoyed.

She had a fire in her step while I was panting like a dazed Rocky Balboa after 15 minutes. It felt kind of humiliating that she drank alcoholic smoothies for breakfast and still was in much better shape than me, a warning signal to lose my morning chocolate croissant. Not that I would, but I considered the signal.

"How are you feeling back there?" B said, likely noticing the increased intensity in my breathing.

"I'm good, I'm good." I lied, trying to sound unaffected. "How are you?" I threw right back at her.

"I feel like I'm in a bad dream and I can't wake up. But otherwise I'm fine." B was in a sour mood which was very hard to reverse. She had been sinking for some time and it finally seemed like she had submerged herself entirely in misery. It would take a heroic effort to dig her up and to be honest with you, I wasn't sure I was up for it.

"Did you fart? Something smells nasty," B said and wrinkled her face in disgust.

"Small one. Sneaked out." I raised my hands in the air to show my innocence.

"You really need to stop eating all that cheese, Darryl, it's not good for you."

Look who's talking! I felt like saying, because I'd be stupid to take health advice from my closet alcoholic employer. And I happened to love my cheese, wine and novel-reading evenings - it might have made my stomach a bit bubbly, but you've got to *live* sometimes, right?

"Did you talk to *A*?" *B*'s voice sounded anxious, but not out of breath. I struggled to keep up with her.

"Yeah, well only a short one, he was polishing his Ferrari." I said, knowing what her reply would be.

"Now that's a surprise!" *B* said. "How much can you

polish a car without it losing its color? He never even drives that thing!"

"A man must have his toys, I guess?" I said, not sure how to defend behavior I couldn't understand, but on the other hand I wasn't particularly experienced when it came to relationships. I had always been a bit of a loner and around women I automatically seemed to land in the friendship category.

"He doesn't seem to care one bit about me anymore. He used to be the nicest husband, always bought flowers, jewelry, did the most romantic things. You remember that time when he brought me up on that skyscraper roof in New York and there was a helicopter waiting for us and we flew to a Caribbean island and had a romantic dinner by the ocean?" *Yes, I remember being left by the helipad like a fool,* I thought to myself and nodded.

B looked out over the rolling hills like the answer to her problem was somewhere over there. Somewhere over the rainbow.

"From flower-petal-trails to scratching his balls openly and only lusting after things with wheels, what an amazing transformation! I used to feel like the most special woman in the world and now I'm like his sister, bucktooth Bree from fucking Oklahoma. I should take a sledgehammer down to that garage!"

What do you say to that? Here was bitterness and disappointment I'd never experienced before, but at the same time expected. The last year they had started to drift apart quite drastically after some major fights and I sometimes wondered how they had made it so far considering how different their personalities were. The banal jock with his cars and protein shakers and the

21

emotional artist with her love for extravagance, yes they were pretty much opposites in everything except for that they were both very, very attractive and successful people. Sometimes that was enough.

At least in the short run.

We jogged the last bit to our regular stretching place and when we stopped I felt like my lungs were trying to launch themselves from my mouth. I was in bad, bad shape. Not fat, but with too much stress, too much wine and not enough exercise. I was maybe a bit unhappy in my own way, not that I had thought about it a lot, but it had slowly started creeping into my head that I might be coming to the end stretch of my employment with *B*. It was becoming too much work and not enough fun.

B was stretching her leg muscles against a rock and I sat down next to her whilst trying to recapture my breath. "You don't think he's retreating to his little man-cave because you've been off the rails lately?" I said, leaning back on my role as the mediator and weirdly seeing it as my duty to make sure the couple stayed together. I knew how happy they could be, it had just been a long time since I saw it.

I looked at *B*'s body and thought to myself how genetically blessed she must be to be able to treat it so badly and still stay so fit and beautiful. She was simply born with that skinny-curvy look that all women want and pay handsomely to get. I couldn't help but feel a tinge of lust.

"You know what I think?" *B* said, looking like she had just thought of something brilliant, "I think he's cheating on me. It would explain everything, the evading behavior, the lack of affection, the night-time jogging, all that. I bet he's been seeing someone for quite a while. You'd tell me if he was, right?" Her stark blue eyes were studying me and for a second I felt like I was in school, trying to invent some believable lie to explain why I hadn't finished my homework. But I didn't have to lie, I knew nothing about *A*'s love life outside *B* and my hunch was that he didn't have any. He just didn't strike me as the cheating kind.

"Why would he cheat on you? You're one of the most beautiful women in the world, according to Maxims and many other magazines, and me, and I know he still thinks you're the love of his life. You just need to work on yourselves and your relationship. It's not the weirdest thing for couples to go through a rough patch."

B looked at me like I was trying to sell her a used car with a bad engine and rust in all the places you couldn't see.

"Thanks for the compliment, Darryl, but that's bullshit. And in a way I can't blame him, I look like a toilet brush. I drink too much, smoke too much, do brainless parts in movies I don't even like myself and go to parties to meet people I don't care one bit about. We haven't had sex in a long time and last time I was barely conscious. Who wouldn't cheat on me?"

"If you're in that self-loathing frame of mind, there's no point in talking anymore." I didn't want to waste time wading around in *B*'s well of depression, I knew it wasn't going to get us anywhere.

"Last question then, if he loves me so god damn much, why isn't he here? Why is he never around?"

I didn't know how to reply. Telling her she was hard work wouldn't cut it, because she knew that already. "I don't know. Maybe you've just hit a rough patch. In Hollywood people sometimes get too stuck in themselves, thinking me, me, me and nothing else and that's why so many marriages crash faster than you have time to say "I do." Your five years is pretty fantastic when you think of it, it must mean you have something really special."

B finally showed me a glimpse of a smile, "How do you do it? How do you always stay so positive?"

"Maybe it's because I don't think so much - guess I'm kind of stupid like that." I flashed my million-dollar smile. I've got REALLY white teeth you know, proud of 'em too.

B looked down on her fingers and then out over the rolling hills and said: "That's it, isn't it? I worry too much and that's why I *needs ma' wine*."

"Something like it. You ought to stop thinking and drinking and your problems will be shrinking."

"You're such a poet, Darryl. All those books you read must do you some good."

"Books over vodka any time, girl," I said and touched her shoulder, "Let's get going again, I think I saw Mr. Gibson walking his dog over there and we don't want you stuck talking to him about how much in common you have."

"Shut up," *B* said and laughed.

I had managed to bring out a sincere smile on her face.

This is why I was her assistant.

***

After our run, *B* wanted a Pinkberry, a non-alcohol indulgence I had no problem with. She donned her oversized shades and I parked the Ranger Rover something like 50 meters from the frozen yoghurt place on a sun-streaked Santa Monica Boulevard. Before heading out, I looked around for paparazzi. To my relief, there were none to be seen, but they were prone to pop-up anywhere at anytime like some evil "jackass-in-a-box". I was just about to walk out when, from the bottom of her cracked confidence, *B* unleashed: "You'd fuck me wouldn't you? If I was single?"

Now what this had to do with frozen yoghurt, I'll never know.

"Yes, I'd pop your Pinkberry if that's what you're talking about. Anyone would, you're smoking hot."

"Thanks, Darryl. Don't you ever quit on me, okay?"

"I promise," I said out of necessity, but it was a promise I knew would be hard to keep.

There was not much of a line in the Pinkberry which was good, because I smelled like locker room and I didn't want to disgust the other customers. The young freckled man behind the counter repeated my order of one Watermelon and one Salted Caramel and gave me a wide smile. For a second I thought he was cross-eyed.

When I was back in the car, *B* dug into her Pinkberry like she had been on a month long Survivor-diet. I have always appreciated women with healthy appetites and I gladly watched her shovel it in.

B of course noticed my big eyes, "What are you looking at? You're staring at me like I'm miss Piggy!"

To which I smiled and said, "I just like to see a woman eat."

"Is that a black man's thing or what? I thought men wanted women who doesn't eat, doesn't talk, fart flowers and who never let anything out of the anus, just into it." B took one more spoon, rolled down the window, threw out the cup and said, "Let's go home, okay?"

"Yeah, let's go before they arrest us for littering." I

replied drily, turned the key and drove off.

On the way home we sat silently in the car, I tried to eat my Pinkberry while managing the steering wheel and *B* was next to me, lost in her own head.

Back at the mansion, she headed off to shower while I went to my office and sat down by the antique desk that *A* got from some celebrity estate for a ridiculously large amount of money. I put my head in my hands and closed my eyes. I felt a heavy weariness set in and knew I was in desperate need of a vacation. Assistants rarely rest and it had started to get to me, much like celebrity life had gotten to *B*. Since I started working for her, I had lost contact with most of my friends and I'd rarely been in touch with my parents. Work, and the glorified world that came with it, had consumed me and I was starting to pay the price.

I probably nodded off for a good twenty minutes, before I was kicked to life by my iPhone dancing on the dark wood. The display read "Julianne".

Julianne was one of those women who had decided to compensate her less fortunate physical appearance by being a ruthless workaholic, determined to put all men down a peg-hole or ten. She had rat-colored hair, a thin mouth and a plank-formed body to go with her sharp, ear-cringing voice that penetrated all sound, and she was the last person I wanted to talk to at that moment. Still, it was my duty to take the call.

"Darryl," I said, praying she would be in a good mood, but I of course knew this wasn't the easiest time to be *B*'s agent, so I expected hell.

"This is one of the biggest fucking PR disasters in Hollywood, Darryl. My phone has been ringing constantly, everybody wants something from her, interviews, statements, appearances, the works but she's refusing to pick up the goddamn phone."

"You know she wants all communication to run through me, I've told you that before, Julianne."

"I don't get it though, why should I have to go through you? I'm *her* agent."

She should have known there was no point in arguing about this, *B* held firm that I was the messenger and her filter to the outside world.

"But why is it so urgent to reach her now? She's in no mood to talk to anyone and I don't see how going on Letterman would make anything better at this stage." I tried to be as firm as I could. You needed to with Julianne.

"This is exactly why I need to talk to her! I've actually started to think that we can spin this in our favor and use the attention to something good."

This is why she was one of the best agents - she saw opportunities everywhere.

"So you're saying she should come out and talk about her problems and in this way redeem herself?" I said, skeptically.

"For once you hit the nail on the head. She needs to take advantage of the publicity, otherwise there is a risk she'll have a tainted image forever. She should talk about how she's battling alcoholism as a result of a tough childhood or whatever the hell she's drinking for. I think we could go for the Oprah book club too, I have some formidable ghostwriters ready to start typing as soon as I give the green light. This doesn't have to be a disaster, but instead a great chance to connect with her fans, show her true, vulnerable self and come out on top. How is she feeling by the way?"

This was a rare show of emotion from Julianne. Maybe she had worked on what she needed to say to sound like an empathic and normal human being.

"She's okay, considering."

"So can I talk to her? I have loads of calls and e-mails I need to return today. If we get started now we can really flip this shit. I know we can!"

Julianne was frighteningly good at her job, but also frighteningly bad at reading people. The chance of *B* going on a talk show at this point in her life was pretty much zero and in a way I felt sorry for Julianne for not understanding this. But you can't blame her for seeing only dollar signs either, it was in her job description.

"I'll talk to her about her options and I'll tell her to call you when she's ready. But right now I think she just wants to rest. I'm pretty sure she's not keen on going on TV to talk about a drinking problem she has hard time admitting to herself. She's really fragile right now."

"Rest is for losers, Darryl. The only thing you should focus on keeping her away from is the bottle, not the spotlight. Hope is not lost if we act fast."

"I'll promise to bring that up when I see her. Thanks."

And Julianne hung up on me without saying goodbye.

***

I want to take a minute to talk about one of the frustrations with living and working in the celebrity world, at least as an assistant. It's the problem to meet women. You see, I used to work all the time, pretty much every day and there wasn't a lot of space for dating. And if I did meet a woman out in a bar or at an event or wherever I might have been, I didn't know where to "conclude" the evening since I was living with the Johnsons and the mansion rule was *not* to bring any outsiders there.

It's pretty logical when you think about it, but once during my first year I broke the role and learned a valuable lesson.

The name of my lesson was Loreena, a chocolate dream with colorful clothing and a big butt to go with it. I love big butts (*and I cannot lie* - as the song goes), always have and always will, so I was of course ecstatic to meet someone like Loreena with a jovial personality, beautiful eyes and two firm watermelon butt cheeks. I was probably too hypnotized by her appearance to realize her ulterior motive for dating me wasn't because she was interested in *me* - like most women she thought I was funny, which is good to draw them in, but apparently not a strong enough incentive in the long run - but because she wanted to get close to the Johnsons. She wasn't a stalker or a lunatic fan or anything like that, but I should have realized something was wrong by how big her eyes grew every time I mentioned them. I of course knew I needed to be careful with yapping about my employers, but when you find someone you like it's not always easy to be modest. Working with celebrities surely helps to make you more interesting. For a while.

In the end, my clouded mind decided it was fine to break a rule and to try and sneak her into the house without anyone seeing her. So one night when my employers were out having one of their romantic candlelight dinners, I brought Loreena up to my room, carefully avoiding other staff members. As soon as we entered the house, Loreena's head was going back and forth with the excitement of a fat kid who had just stepped inside the Charlie Chocolate factory, while I was preoccupied with not being seen. She soon followed her deranged look up with questions about the Johnsons - where in the house they stayed, where they were right that minute, what my relationship with them was like, what a typical day would look like for them and so on. I had answered some of them before, but here they came again at an alarming rate of brain-diarrhea. A voice in my head started telling me that these questions had nothing to do with me, but her huge, juicy butt completely obstructed my otherwise logical thought-process.

Loreena ended up spending the night in my bed, but when I woke up at five in the morning by my bladder calling me, she wasn't there. I knew I wasn't a Casanova, but could the sex have been *that* bad? It was hard for me to place an objective judgement on it, especially since it was over in a couple of minutes.

I dressed in my shorts and Nuke "Just Done It" t-shirt and went out to look for her. I walked downstairs and I was so tired I almost slipped on the marble stairs, polished into a death trap by an eager Elena. I walked around quietly not to wake the other staff members and was just about to text her when I spotted her and her chubby ass sneaking around by the pool. *What the hell?* I thought, got myself over there and started wheezing: "Loreena! Loreena!" When her face finally turned my way she looked like a deer caught in the headlights of car. For a second I thought she would try to run away or something equally crazy, but instead she came up to me and said with a slight quiver in her voice, "I was just taking a walk around the house."

"A walk around the house? I saw you, that wasn't *walking*, it was *sneaking* around! I implicitly told you not to be seen! You could land me in a lot of trouble you know."

"I couldn't sleep and wanted to take a look around. Relax a little will you?" Like an attacked animal, Loreena thought the best defensive was offensive. I didn't care a whole lot for her tone.

"Relax? This is my job on the line, how can you tell me to relax?"

And then I saw it. The necklace she definitely *wasn't* wearing the night before. It was a butterfly in gold and blue stone and looked far too expensive to be hanging around Loreena's neck, if you know what I'm saying.

"What's that around your neck?" I glared at Loreena, my adrenaline at a peak. The date was rapidly becoming a very bad idea.

"It's a necklace. I had it in my bag."

"That's *B*'s necklace! You're a liar *and* a thief!"

I could see in her face how Loreena was waging an internal war; it was a gated property so making a run for it wasn't an option.

"Ah, fuck you, Darryl! I just wanted some glamour in my life! I wanted to see a celebrity, maybe wear an expensive necklace for a little while! Would she care about one little necklace? They have millions, billions!"

I was impressively calm considering the situation and told her: "Give me the necklace back and I won't call the police. It's time to go home."

That was the only time I brought a girl to the mansion. This didn't make me a monk, but I would have been lying if I said I was close to a meaningful relationship with any other woman than *B*.

Slugs got more action.

And *B* was, like you know by now, not herself. When it came to the many good times we had shared together, I had to rely almost only on older memories.

Speaking of which, I do recall many great moments, often ending in massive fits of laughter since humor was our strongest denominator. While I'm taking a stroll down memory lane, I can't help but smile and think about the cover shoot in Paris, ridiculously romantic with the sun going down behind a beautiful French 15th century castle, and the hilariously parodic photographer, stereotypically complete with a comical Anglo-French accent, a t-shirt-blazer-scarf-combo, unruly hair and his dark-haired assistant Annelié, silent, but cute and making lots of eye contact with me. I returned the looks from time to time, when I wasn't watching the French bastard give *B*, for the shoot dressed in a rather slinky Arabian Nights-inspired outfit, directions to a better pose. *Is all that touching really necessary?* I remember thinking.

The moment, the setting, the atmosphere, everything is so sharply carved into my memory tree that I can summon it in an instant, close my eyes and travel there like Scotty on the Starship Enterprise.

For a second I thought *B* was charmed by Pierre, giggling too much, giving him her famous flirtatious smile. I was jealous and worried about her, but then I noticed Annelié again; her dark eye-brows, small head, beautiful chestnut eyes and I lost concentration.

There was a pool not far from where we were standing. A glorious, lit swimming pool, fit for a king.

Fit for a Pierre.

And then, during our break, it happened. Pierre was walking towards the catering section, head leaned backwards, his long, slightly wet-looking hair, bouncing behind him. He held his huge camera casually in one hand

and was taking large, relaxed strides towards us, looking like a guy so sure of himself it was ridiculous, while we were standing at a white bar table, drinking a glass of wine and admiring the view. He called something out to Annelié, who was hovering around us again, a bit too shy to talk but eager with the eyes. I think she preferred to look at anything but Pierre, who treated her like she was the Ringer of Notre Dame and not the petite and beautiful woman she was.

On the floor there was a light cable that I had stepped over a couple of times, carefully avoiding a slip and a tumble. But Pierre had his eyes to the sky and managed to put his pointy patent-leather shoe under the wire, got snagged in it and fell backwards, the camera left his hand (all this happened in slow motion) and I saw Annelié somehow managing to catch it, but nobody was catching Pierre, he was tumbling, slipping and with a *splash* he was in the pool.

There's no way you could witness this and hold back laughter and we all laughed so hard we cried. Even Annelié. Poor Pierre was in the pool, soaked, miserable and humiliated. I don't know if I'd been able to see the fun in it, being in the water, but the Frenchman for sure couldn't. He looked like he had put his face in a bowl of sour cream and cancelled the rest of the shoot.

B and I laughed about the pool incident the whole evening (*A* was filming in Germany) and we still think back to it at times, and talk about Pierre with the accent, Pierre the stereotyped French artist, Pierre in the swimming pool.

But that was the past and the past was *past* and no matter how much of a golden shimmer you add to it in your memory bank (using some mental photoshopping), you can't live there. You need to live in the *present* and that was what I intended to do.

***

After a piping hot shower, I headed down to the kitchen for lunch and chef Jorge's famous tuna salad. I sat down by the kitchen island and Jorge, who looked weirdly forlorn, placed the plate in front of me in haste. His tuna salad was the tastiest way to cut the carbs and it was something I needed to do badly. I never had the rock-solid, action hero body with visible abs and I was fine with that, but I was still concerned about how soft and doughy the skin around my midsection had become. I was nearing 30 and part of me was terrified it was all going to be downhill from there. My indulgences were few, the previously mentioned chocolate croissant, the half bottle of wine with dinner and possibly a slice of cheese or three afterwards, but still every digested gram seemed to count.

But eating Jorge's salad wasn't a huge concession, he usually put the exact amount of dressing and seasoning and always used the freshest vegetables and the best tuna he could find. It was a treat. Usually.

This time though, something was wrong with it. It was overly vinegary, bordering towards sour and the first mouthful made me cringe. I struggled through a few bites and then pushed the plate aside. I walked out of the kitchen and found Jorge sitting on a chair in the back garden looking like a ton of bricks just had fallen on him.

"What's up?" I asked.

"You didn't like it did you?"

"What?"

"The tuna salad. You didn't like it." Jorge gave me a look telling me there was no point in lying. Everything about him was big, his body, his face, his heart and his mind and he knew very well that I didn't like it.

"I don't know, there was something a bit different with it today, I guess." I said, knowing how much his cooking meant to him.

Jorge rose from the chair quickly, removed his chef's hat, ran his left hand through his curly patch of hair and said: "Darryl, I botched it. The dressing. The cap came off and you know? Too much." It seemed like to Jorge there was more than a tuna salad at stake here.

"Don't worry, Jorge. It's a salad. I'll survive. What else is wrong?"

Jorge looked at me with his big brown eyes and then let them travel out into the garden as if they were more comfortable there, and said, "It's my son, Luís. He isn't doing well in school anymore, his grades are off, he's having troubles focusing, his teachers are concerned. When I ask him about it, he says he wants to be an RnB singer and couldn't care less about school. It's very upsetting."

A young person in LA struck by the fame-drug, didn't sound too rare to me, but finding a cure was more difficult though. Once the desire for an exuberant existence gets into your brain, it seems to develop much like a virus, soon taking over your whole being. It becomes difficult to focus on anything else than finding a way to the spotlight. I don't have any research or stats to prove it, but I've seen it up close.

I tried to soften the blow, "Well it's good to have a dream and a drive to achieve it. Does he have any actual talent?"

"I know it sounds harsh, but I don't think so. His

interest in music started rather late, too late if you ask me. Or maybe I just don't get what he's trying to do. I'm afraid he's throwing his life away trying to be the next MTV sensation."

"I haven't heard him and I doubt I ever will by the sound of it, but I agree with your thinking. It will be hard to break it to him though, it sounds like his desire is firmly rooted."

Jorge shook his giant head and reached over and touched the stem of a pink flower very gently, like it was a sacred object, "It worries me, the way he's wasting his time only setting himself up to get hurt. I wish he could put all that energy somewhere else. In education, a serious profession. My family never had the money to study and get a degree and the one who finally gets the chance, is suddenly eager to throw it all away. It breaks a father's heart."

"The world puts a lot of pressure on the young, Jorge." I said, still counting myself among the world's young and feeling the pressure. "Besides, you're a celebrity chef, well at least a celebrity-hired chef, so my guess is he would want to do something big, as not to disappoint you."

"He wouldn't disappoint me even if he decided to work at McDonalds for the rest of his life. The important thing is he's happy, that's all I care about."

"But maybe that's not all *he* cares about? I think sometimes parents make the mistake to think that whatever their children do or want, they had something to do with it. And besides, trying out a music career might make him really happy, no matter how silly it may sound to you."

Jorge appeared to consider this odd piece of wisdom, coming from a much younger guy with no experience in parenting whatsoever. But everyone's free to have opinions and I'm kind of keen to throw mine around sometimes.

"True," he said, but I could tell he wasn't entirely sure about my reasoning, "How's B by the way?"

"Better now, but obviously not great. I'd say she'd love some comfort food today, but I'm not sure her body needs it."

"I'll see what I can do. I won't make her a tuna salad, that's for sure." Jorge finally gave me a smile, which was nice to see. He was generally a very happy camper and I really disliked seeing him worry like this.

"Just go easy on the dressing and you'll be fine. I'm going to run back to the office now. I'll think if there's something we can do about your son. Does he have a website or a Myspace page or something where I can check him out?"

"I don't know actually, but I doubt it. What's Myspace?"

"It doesn't matter, I'll google him. Thanks for lunch, Jorge."

"It was nothing. And I mean it this time."

***

I didn't see B for the rest of the day. She had told me she wanted to stay unreachable and I forwarded the message to Julianne. I couldn't blame her for wanting to shut the world out, a day after vomiting all over it. I sat down and looked at the upcoming scheduling, the month was going to be rather quiet, she had a few meetings booked about upcoming roles, a short interview with Vogue on her dress sense and one appearance at some celebrity fundraiser for green energy. I wondered how long she would feel like

37

hiding from the spotlight, would we need to cancel everything or would she walk out of her room like a new being, ready to forget about the whole thing and start anew? Despite working closely with her for years, I couldn't really know, because we had never faced this kind of pickle before. Not that she was easy to read from the start - she would better be described as an emotional tsunami. When she was happy, she was phenomenal to be around, and when she was sad or angry, difficult was an understatement. With B, everything came in extremes and you had to take the good with the bad.

I poured myself a glass of wine and contemplated possible causes for her recent destructive behavior. I spun around in my leather chair and sipped the lukewarm liquid and let it fill me with goodness. Wine had become such a passion over the years, a passion I desperately hoped to turn into a dream one day, opening my own wine bar. I put a slice of brie cheese in my mouth and thought back to brighter days. It was hard to pin down exactly what had happened to B since I entered her life, maybe things had just caught up with her? She sometimes complained about the industry and how she had been pinned into one category of roles and films and how frustrated she was with never being able to show her true range, but it was difficult to see her career as bad enough to make her feel like a train-wreck. Surely there must be something more, something deeper.

There were her parents of course. Her "unloving" (B's wording) mother Katherine who had pushed her to the top, taken a slice of the cake and then left her there and who only seemed to have harsh words for her own daughter. And her father who had gone away when B was three years old, leaving a big dent in her upbringing and making her seek the approval she could never get because of his death in a car accident, six or seven years ago. He had been a painter who had gotten tired of diaper-changes and screaming and decided to move to France and become a full-time - but never famous or successful - artist. *B* had been left with her troubled mother and it must have made its mark, although for some reason she wouldn't admit it to herself. She was strangely too proud to seek any kind of counseling or therapy and her stubbornness had, to my mind, proven to be mentally costly. For all of us.

So parents, career troubles and fading fortunes in her marriage - not a cocktail to celebrate with. The marriage problems could probably be traced to one big thing, her reluctance to bring a child into the world. Her husband had been on her for years and tried all his might to convince her, but to no avail. Although she was emotionally rather unstable, at the same time she wasn't easily swayed.

There were, to summarize, many reasons *B*'s boat was rather rocky and maybe the vomit incident gave it its final push and tumble.

***

Interlude

Before I forget, it might make sense to mention how I became such a wine nerd. It will prove relevant, so bear with me (but if you hate back-story you can skip it).

In my happy and worry-free 20s, my best friend Cesar and I decided to go on a European road trip, driving through several cities of Britain, France, Spain, Italy,

Austria, and Germany in an old, yellow Mercedes which we bought second hand outside Hamburg from a fat and mustached man for next to nothing. We had saved up for years, me working for my father's building business and Cesar setting up basic websites for small companies, something he called "computer whoring".

It was during our stop in Italy that I had my first date with a beautiful wine. I was mostly a beer drinker then, at least in the capacity a young man in D.C. could get a hold of the stuff (21-year-age limit). I didn't really know anything about wine and the few glasses I'd tried were sour and vinegary. But when we reached the region of Tuscany and our ugly and battered Mercedes broke down just outside the city of Sienna, this changed forever. While we had our car in for repair with a guy in dusty blue coveralls who just couldn't stop smoking, we rented an ugly old room with moldy curtains in the first cheap little hotel we could find and hit the streets.

Sienna is a time machine. It's like you walked straight into medieval times with its narrow cobblestone streets and leaning brick buildings and the feeling of history is so strong you wouldn't be surprised to see a knight in shining armor pass you on the street. We decided to enjoy it Italian style and ordered a platter in a small restaurant on a side street, but the waiter didn't have anything besides the yeasty local beer, which we didn't like, so he recommended a bottle of Tuscan wine. I remember the first sip like yesterday, it hit my taste buds like lightning and filled my whole being with a sense of, I don't know, *romance? Lust? Desire?*

It was simply love at first taste.

We ended up finishing the bottle and then another and

the owner seemed so happy to have us there he gave us a tour of his wine cellar and started explaining the differences between certain wines and grapes and although my head was starting to get sore, I sucked most of it in like an anteater.

So that was how the dream was formed to have my own wine bar, or *enoteca* as the Italians call it, a place where customers and other wine enthusiasts can relax in comfortable chairs, enjoy an exquisite glass of wine and listen to some soft live jazz or a classical violinist pouring his soul into a Bach partita. A haven for the cultured.

Yes, you could say I'm a bit of a snob.

***

The alarm clock woke me at half past six the next day. I stared at it with incredulous eyes, trying to figure out how it got there so fast and why I had a feverish burn inside my head. It didn't take me long to realize the culprit was one glass of wine too many. That *Brunello* was simply far too good for comfort.

After a quick shower which did little to mitigate the pain in my membrane, I headed downstairs, desperate for my morning espresso.

There was a shaking sound coming from the kitchen, *slosh, slosh, slosh. Slosh, slosh, slosh*. The sound was quickly explained by me laying eyes on *A*, jerking a plastic red protein shaker.

"Morning," he said, in a somber voice which was unnatural to his usually bright and cheerful self.

"Morning. You sound down?" I mumbled. Too early. No coffee.

"We had a huge fight last night. Huge. She took a suitcase and left." He stopped shaking his drink and studied the content, which had become a grey-brownish soil. I wondered how the protein people could call that *chocolate* when "sewage" seemed more apt.

"Oh, that bad?" I said, not feeling too surprised, as it wasn't the first time *B* had made a dramatic exit and gone to spend the night at a friends' house. It was an obvious attempt to elicit emotion from *A*, but she had complained that it only seemed to work for a day or two and then he went back to being the frosty caveman again.

Who said love was easy?

"My guess is she's with Katie, but I've no idea really. She refuses to pick up her phone." *A* put the shaker against his mouth and let the foul liquid run down his throat. I looked away briefly and thought he might be right, Katie always had a good ear for *B*'s problems, meaning she agreed with pretty much everything the movie star said or felt.

A made a disgusting swallowing sound and said, "Can you do me favor and check if she's okay? I was a bit tough yesterday, said some things I regret."

"Well, that happens in a fight, I guess. What did you say?"

"I told her she was a selfish, alcoholic psycho with major issues. And I told her I'm soon giving up on having kids, I'm turning 40, it's already quite late to start a family."

Bringing up the old *our-fantastic-genes-force-us-to-procreate* discussion after *B*'s social disaster wasn't the best timing, but you couldn't really blame him for hearing the clock ticking. Extending the family was the natural next step, together with divorce of course. I thought they had reached some kind of tipping point where relationships either made it or broke it. I had seen it before with friends, but never gotten as far myself.

"Can you please make sure she's okay? I really have to go now." *A* gave me a look that said he knew I would say yes, after all, it was my job to be the yes-man. I was paid for it.

"Sure thing," I said and thought how strange it was to have another man ask you to manage his marriage. Being a relationship middleman was never in my contract, but it became a vital part of my job the last year of my employment. Question was, was it possible to save it? At that moment I thought it wasn't very likely.

"You're the man, Darryl. I don't know what I would do without you. I'll call you from New York, okay?"

And as *A* left to finish his packing, I turned on the espresso machine, letting it slowly chug out a thick, luscious brew. I took my first sip and thought that I didn't know what he'd do without me either.

***

A marriage without fights can't be a healthy one, but when the fights outnumber the moments of peace, you'd probably start to wonder what the hell you're doing.

The Johnsons had reached this stage and therefore I wasn't shocked *not* to hear from *B* for the whole next day. She had gone to hide from agent Julianne, the paparazzi, her marriage struggles, her mother, her disappointing career, yes pretty much everything that upset her. It wasn't the most mature thing to do, but you can't go around being mature all the time, right?

So I figured I should let her take her time and not chase

her. Besides, it gave me well-needed break from work. I hadn't had much time off the last two years and a heavy tiredness had started to creep into my bones.

But after almost two whole days of rest without a word from *B*, I started to wonder and sent her a text. No reply. I gave her a call. No reply. I gave her another call a bit later. No reply. The feeling that something was wrong had started to infiltrate my brain like a small but pounding headache. I actually ended up calling Katie, Alice, her mother Katherine, everyone I could think of, but no one had heard from her.

I deliberated calling *A* for a moment but decided it would just worry him and ultimately piss him off. He was directing a movie for the first time in his career and it was not the best time to disturb him.

But how do you locate a missing celebrity? There are surely no phone apps for it and if there isn't a phone app, then what? A thought hit me that I should call the police, but somehow it seemed too dramatic, too soon. It could still just be stubbornness, maybe she was holing up in a hotel somewhere in the city, eating buckets of ice cream and watching Sex and the City?

I heard a *pling* sound from my Macbook. My best friend, IT-genius and European tour travel buddy was writing to me on Skype. I hadn't talked to him in a week so it was a welcome distraction.

"Yo," the message eloquently read. Cesar wasn't elaborate with words, he preferred to get to the point quickly and his speech was often infused with slang and profanity. He was a super-intelligent and baby-faced goofball with a Rastafari hairstyle and I feared he'd never grow up. He had inherited a small loft in New York and

44

worked for a mobile game developer. This was taking the easy way out for Cesar, who probably had enough computer skills to work for NASA and could hack pretty much any website out there. But hacking websites was not the best way to make a living as he had learned from experience. And police.

"Hey," I wrote back.

"What's up?"

"Panic mode. *B* is missing. They had a fight two days ago and she took her bags and left. Nobody knows where she is."

"I could see that."

"What do you mean?"

"I read about her vomit. Anyone would run away from that sort of thing."

"You can say that again," I wrote and put a sad smily at the end of it.

"If you want I can try and trace her. All I need is her credit card details."

My heart stopped for a minute. Why hadn't I thought of this? She must have made some kind of transaction in three days and it might at least give me a clue. On the other hand I didn't feel comfortable giving out her credit card number to one of the most money-horny people I knew. He was my best friend, but Cesar and money was always a dangerous equation.

But then again, what choice did I have?

"Okay, wait and I'll give them to you. Don't lose them or use them for something else, okay?"

"Of course not. And send a text message. It's safer."

Luckily, I had her card details in an old e-mail which she had sent to use in case I needed to buy something online. This was before they gave me my own expense card which gold-ish sheen I treasured and admired greatly.

I felt a second of regret before I pushed the send-button. "How long does it take?" I wrote to him.

"Not too long. Give me an hour and I'll call you."

"Thanks, man," I wrote and headed down to the kitchen to make a sandwich, hoping my decision wouldn't prove costly.

Down in the kitchen I found Elena cleaning the floor. She had her permanently disappointed facial expression on and I knew she wouldn't try to start up a conversation. She rarely did. I silently wondered what her plan was, she was nearing 60 and was still working as hard as ever. I didn't know much about her, only that she came from small-town Russia with her son twenty years ago and that he was struggling to find a job as an actor (and enjoying the LA party life a little too much), while she was making floors shine in already successful actors' homes. It was maybe not what she had imagined when she came here, but I wouldn't know, as we had never talked about her feelings. Her skinny and veiny body did all the talking as the broom squished across the marble floors.

I took a bite out of my ham and cheese sandwich and pretended to read the newspaper, while I was really too anxious to focus on anything. I wanted Cesar to call me and tell me where *B* was so I could move on with my life and do other things. It was while sitting at the kitchen bar that I realized how much I cared about her. I always knew we had a bond, a friendship, some kind of chemistry, but my feelings had never been tested like this before. One minute I wanted to quit and the next I felt so sorry for her, that it felt like I could *never* leave her.

So it was with a sinking feeling in my stomach that I heard the phone vibrate on the table. The display read "Cesar". I jumped on it like a cat on a light reflection.

"What have you got?" I burst out.

"Not even hello? LA broke your manners, dude. Anyway, her last transaction was at a restaurant, a *La Rosetta*. In Rome."

"In Rome?!" My mind went numb for a second. This was apparently trouble on an international scale.

"Yes, the two previous transactions also happened in Rome. So my guess is that's where she is, unless someone stole her credit card."

"Oh, shit!" Cesar exclaimed, before I got the chance to reply.

"What? What is it?" My heart was now ready to unleash itself from my chest, which was far from my usually quite a cool character.

"Crazy lady spent 1300 dollars. 1300 dollars in a restaurant!"

I sighed a breath of relief, "Believe me, on this level of fame, it's not that much."

"Are you kidding? That's almost a month's rent and I live in New York."

"So you're positive she's there? In Rome?" This was a new level of *B*'s spontaneity, so I had to make sure.

"I bet you 500 dollars."

"If you're right, I'd owe you big time. This is nuts. I have to call her husband now, thanks for being the C in CSI."

"CSI is some bullshit."

It was a shame I couldn't stay on the phone with Cesar, because we hadn't talked in a while, but I had bigger fish to fry and husbands to call. It took about ten rings before *A* picked up his phone. He didn't strike me as over-eager to hear about where his wife went, but maybe it was my imagination.

A didn't have even a hint of a clue of why B had decided to visit the capital of Italy. She had been there only once before, two years ago for a cover shoot, he remembered, but he didn't know anything beyond that. Then he said something which hit me hard.

"You have to go."

"What?"

"You need to go to Rome and talk to her, Darryl. I can't do it, I've got a movie to finish. And you've got this friend of yours to help you too. It's the only solution."

"You seriously want me to fly to another continent and track her down? I've called her like twenty times, she's not answering. It's not going to be easy, because she obviously doesn't want to be found."

"It's the best we can do. I'll pay you extra, whatever you need. I really need you to do this, you seem like the only one who can talk some sense into her."

It's not great when your husband thinks the only guy who can talk to you, is some other guy, in this case me. But I knew he was right. If anyone had a chance of reaching out to B it was yours truly and that's why I couldn't give him no for an answer either. And not only for his sake, but for B's sake and mine, as I was genuinely worried about her.

Not that Rome was the worst place to go celebrity hunting either.

I packed my bags as fast as I could, checked the flights online and bought a last-minute ticket with my glimmering expense card. It was going to be one impromptu trip, but I have to admit I was a bit excited to go to Rome a second time. I thought it might be the break I needed, even if it was going to involve some kind of detective work. I ran down the shining marble staircase and at the end I almost bumped into Elena.

"See where you going," she muttered in her sour voice.

"I'm flying to Rome. *B* is there. Why I don't know." I burst out.

Elena shook her head and sighed, "I know she run away. Her husband never home and she drink like animal. Not happy relationship." She stabbed a finger at me like I was responsible for the whole thing. This was as animated as I'd ever seen her.

"I'll call you when we're coming back," I said and I was out the door before Elena had a chance to reply.

***

Rome hadn't changed much from my journey there ten years ago, it was still picturesque, the people beautiful, the coffee fantastic and the wines made you want to practice the ancient religion of alcoholism. The city's amazing heritage led you to expect an architectural wonder every time you turned the corner on the worn cobblestone streets. I knew I could live there if I learned the language, that's how connected I feel to the Roman look on life, with their food, wine, music and women. It wasn't hard to see why *B* had picked this as her escape route.

Thanks to Cesar and his persistent follow-up on her transactions, I already had a great clue when I landed. Her credit cards indicated that she was staying at Hotel Hassler, an impeccable five-star hotel on top of the famous Spanish steps. It was a beautiful spring day in Rome and although the flight had been long and I was tired like a dog, the excitement of being back in one of my favorite cities brought me some extra energy.

I hailed a cab and when I sat down in the car and told him the address of the hotel, I felt very calm all of a sudden, like I knew things would work out. In all seriousness they didn't look great at that stage. What would happen when I found *B*? She wouldn't suddenly be all happy and ready to work on her relationship and the world would still not have forgotten about the vomit and suddenly be ready to land her major roles in epic dramas. Things were far from easy.

I thought back to Cesar always giving me crap for my job, saying it wasn't really dignified to be an "assistant", his immature feedback being that he would never get a job with "ass" in it. I knew I should take him with a pinch of salt, especially since he thought the whole celebrity world was ridiculous - a figment of crazy people's imagination - and thought higher of me and my abilities, but sometimes I couldn't help but think that four years was a long time to be someone's assistant. I wanted more.

After the driver had dropped me off at the hotel, I decided to walk over to the steps and look at the crowd in the *Piazza di Spagna*. The square was crowded and the slanting steps leading up to where I was standing were full of street merchants and tourists, just taking a break in the sun. Life in Rome seemed simple.

I turned around to walk to the hotel across the street from me, when something unexpected happened.

An evil-looking black Lamborghini drove up with a screech in front of me, and suddenly, like it all happened in a split second, a stylishly dressed woman in a navy-inspired dress, high-heels and over-sized shades walked out from the hotel at the same time a man in long black hair and a pinstriped suit climbed out of the Lamborghini and opened the door (upwards) for her. She smiled at him like they were old friends and sat down inside the shining monster of a car. All this happened before I realized...it was *B*!

I stood there dumbstruck for a while and when my brain finally jolted to life, it was too late too shout her name and the car was already speeding away from me with a scream, leaving me standing there wondering what the hell I'd just witnessed.

That instant I felt anger rise up through me: anger at *B* for making me chase her to a foreign country just to see her drive away with her lover. Anger for how relaxed she looked, while I worried like crazy. Anger at how stupid it had been of me to miss her.

***

I did the only reasonable thing after that experience and got myself a room at The Hassler. The receptionist looked quite happy to slide my credit card in her little machine and empty it from hundreds of euro. I was happy too, because it wasn't my money and the hotel looked absolutely amazing. I was obviously getting used to this kind of standard after four years, but I tried to remind myself to really enjoy it every time, because it's when you start to take things for granted that you lose them.

While I filled up a foamy bath in my room I noticed a twinge of jealousy creaking in my bones. I felt like *B* wasn't only cheating on her husband, but on me too, breaking some kind of unspoken promise and hurting our friendship.

My brain churned like a tired engine, trying to think of

ways to break this to *A* as objectively as possible. But I needed to talk to *B* first, we were closer friends after all and there was an iota of a chance she wasn't really sleeping with the suave-looking spaghetti stallion. For some reason the whole thing made me think of my parents, who had created and lived such a stable life in Arlington, Virginia for over 30 years, a life so different from the Hollywood lifestyle I was in the middle of. A part of me had always wanted what they had - the predictability of knowing what's going to happen tomorrow and the day after and being able to rely on a steady rhythm of life - while another part of me found it horribly boring. There was a reason I was in Hollywood; I was looking for action, excitement and larger-than-life experiences - I wanted the unexpected. Despite coming from a humble background and a quiet, comfortable upbringing, I liked the idea of looking life in the eye and asking it: "What have you got?"

But this extramarital drama was not my cup of tea.

Waiting for *B* to return to the hotel was a tiresome job and as I browsed around the TV channels looking for something to catch my eye or at least keep it open, I felt my body get heavier and heavier, like I was slowly sinking through the soft mattress. It had been a long flight, an exhausting day and no matter how hard I fought it, the inevitable happened and I fell asleep.

It was one of those sleeps that when you wake up, you feel like you've been cocooning for months like some weird insect. My head was thick as a brick and my mouth was dry. I sat up in bed and for a second I didn't know where I was and what time it was. I looked around the room, saw that the TV was on, an Italian farce playing with lots of screaming and giggling, and I wondered how I could fall asleep to that. On the table were leftovers from my room service dinner and half a bottle of Chianti. Everything slowly came back to me and because it was ten to two in the morning, I figured *B* must be back from her nighttime adventures. The only way to find out, I figured, was to head up to her room.

I knocked three times on the wooden penthouse door and waited with my heart in my stomach for some kind of reply, but there was only the growling of my belly. I knew I needed to resign myself to the fact that she might actually be cuddling with a piece of male *penne,* without any intention whatsoever of heading back to her room. I sighed deeply and pressed the glossy elevator button to go down again. It took a very long time. I thought maybe the elevator was stuck somewhere between floors and I was just about to give up and take the stairs when the doors opened and I had the shock of my life.

Standing in the elevator, him with a dazed look on his face and her leaning on his shoulder, was *B* and her macho man.

"*B!*" I cried out and she jolted to life. She opened her eyes, stretched her arms upwards, walked out from the elevator and threw her arms around me. "*Darryyyyylll! How come you'rrreee herrree?*" she said with a breath that could double as insecticide.

I glanced over at her man-friend and he gave me a disappointed look, telling me I had been there just in time to ruin a possibly nice finish to the evening for him. At least if he was into unconscious movie stars.

"Let's go to your room and I'll tell you," I said, remarkably stern and focused for being so exhausted and surprised at the same time.

After she dismissed the Italian stud with a long hug and a kiss on the cheek, I helped *B* stumble her way into the penthouse, where she laid down in her bed and gave out a loud, toxic burp. I could feel my eyes itch from tiredness, but I was still more attractive than she was at that point in time, which was a first. I should have had a photo taken.

I sat down next to her on the bed, leaving some space between us, in case she was ready for another projectile vomit. I was still angry with her and had loads of questions about the *Italiano* steaming in my brain.

Like she anticipated how I felt, she said, "You hate me don't you?"

"No, of course I don't hate you. I was just worried about you, because the *B* I know doesn't run away to foreign countries to have late night rendezvous' with other men."

B looked down on her hands, like they were somehow to blame for everything. "I'm sorry, but I had to get away. My marriage, the vomit, it was a new low. I couldn't stand to look people in the face anymore." She sounded remarkably sober for...being *B*.

"I understand that, we all do. But you could still have told me, I didn't think we had any secrets between each other. It's a bit silly that I have to chase you down in Rome like some kind of private detective. You didn't answer the phone so I had to track you through your credit card, can you believe that? And another thing, who is that guy? You do remember that no matter how shitty you feel about your marriage, you're still married, right?"

"I'm not sleeping with Matteo! We're friends. And I'm sorry you had to come all the way here and that I didn't answer my fucking phone and that I'm such a mess, but I really don't need you to judge me either. Everybody's already doing a swell job of that."

B was coming alive while I was starting to feel my weariness again. I had found her and completed my mission and all I wanted at that moment was to go back to sleep. We could deal with all the drama and questioning later.

And like she was reading my mind, it was exactly what *B* intended to do too. "We'll continue this talk tomorrow," *B* said and closed her eyes.

I sat on the side of the bed like a parent, until she snored and then I started arranging the pillows for myself on the penthouse sofa.

***

I woke up to find the sun peeking through the window, hinting about another beautiful day in the eternal city. My lower back ached from spending the night on the small and stiff sofa, but I saw it as a small price to pay to find that *B* was in fact alright and that she hadn't been up to any coital activities with her dark, Italian friend. I looked over at *B* who lay there in her large bed, clothes still on, hair frazzled, make-up smudged in her face and completely unaware that I was there, watching her. She was a mess, but somehow still managed to pull it off, the way attractive women could with just about anything.

I took a long shower, one where it felt like I was getting rid of dirt that had lodged itself in cavities I didn't know I had. When I stepped out, I was dry as a prune, but refreshed, looking forward to spending the day with *B* while trying to understand what was going on in that beautiful but confused head of hers.

My spirits rose as I sat down outside on the massive

terrace, the sun gazing at me and a cup of warming instant coffee in my hand. The view was spectacular from up there, where you could see Rome open up with all its beautiful domes and buildings and I couldn't help but feel a wave of joy to be there again. I sipped my coffee and wondered what would happen, if we would go back to LA, if she would like to stay in Rome or even go to New York to see her husband and make amends. They were all possibilities and with *B* it was almost impossible to figure out what she had in mind until she told you.

Suddenly I felt a presence behind me and I turned around to see a zombie, imitating B, standing there in her clothes from yesterday and looking absolutely miserable.

"Morning," she said, in coarse voice.

"Morning," I replied.

She sat down opposite me by the outdoor table and buried her head in her hands, "Why, oh, why, oh, why do I drink?" she said loudly, the last part almost coming out as a cry.

"To get away from yourself maybe?" I said, casually and poured her a cup of coffee.

"I think I need a proper breakfast, some fats, bacon, eggs, cheese, the works." *B* said, still covering her face and ignoring my comment, "I didn't eat much last night."

"If you can eat now you can't feel *that* bad. Will the heart attack breakfast package be suitable for madame?" I said and could sense a smile before I walked inside to call room service.

B took a shower while we waited for the breakfast guy. She came out of the bathroom looking less like a zombie and more like a beautiful girl with rosy cheeks and wet hair in need of a good comb.

"That was nice," she said, while drying her hair with a monogrammed hotel towel.

"You look less dead now," I replied and smiled.

"You're such a sweetie, Darryl."

Breakfast came on a large rolling tray pushed by a guy in a bright red uniform, curly black hair and a thin mustache. He smelled of cheap spray deodorant and stared at *B* like all starstruck people do. I gave him a look that said "*yeah, it's her*" and handed him a ten euro bill in tip.

I picked up a croissant and looked at it like it was a bitter enemy. In one way it was, I have never been good at saying no to pastries and being in a country that prided itself on food wasn't going to be easy.

B put her fork through a fried egg and snatched it between her teeth like some kind of jungle cat. She could eat like a pig if she wanted to, so I was lucky the breakfast was large enough to feed four starving body-builders.

We were both quiet for a while, going at the food like it was an Olympic event. After my second cup of coffee I decided it was time, since my belly rumbled and I could be running to the bathroom soon. Big breakfasts and coffee did this to me.

"So the guy's just a friend?" I said, it coming out a bit more tense than I expected. I didn't want a fight, I just had some annoying curiosity to kill.

"Yes, he is. We met at that film-shoot two years ago where he managed the wardrobe. I think you were in the hospital then?"

"Yeah," I said and thought back to when I was hit from behind at a red light by a senile lady with blue hair. I ended up getting a bad whiplash injury and couldn't go to Rome with *B*. She never told me about this guy though, which concerned me.

"I know you might think he's gay because he's in fashion or whatever, but he looked very into you from the 30 seconds I saw of him."

B gave me a deadpan look. She thought I was clueless about these things. In a way I was.

"Believe me, he's gay. A woman knows. You feel it."

"How do you feel that? He didn't get a boner when he hugged you or what?"

"You're such a lovely conversational partner, Darryl. Do I ever tell you that?" She said, and at first she looked really angry with me, for which I wouldn't blame her, but then she started laughing and I started laughing too.

It was the best moment we've had in a while and I felt a glimmer of hope that the real *B* could come back.

If she wanted to.

***

After breakfast we decided to take a long walk. With the six-hour time difference, it was still too early to call *A* and tell him the good news, so we had some hours together to just enjoy the city and do what we did best, which was talk.

"Imagine if I could walk the streets this unnoticed back in LA? How different my life would be." *B* said from behind her big sunglasses.

I noticed many people give her an extra look-over so I was pretty sure she was exaggerating her escape from the public light, but at the same I understood how good it must feel for her to walk around for a while without a group of camera-carrying buzzards circling around her.

"You would like to be less famous? I thought a big part

of you loved it?"

"I don't know, it's up and down. I guess part of me really likes being seen and analyzed constantly, it's something I've wanted ever since I was a little kid. Maybe it's some kind of residue from being an only child or maybe it's just what everybody wants."

"I'm also an only child, but I don't think I ever wanted the spotlight or fame."

"And that's why you're in Hollywood, working with me?" B gave me a smirk like *you must be kidding*.

"Good point," I said and smiled back.

We walked until our feet hurt and went for a late lunch at a restaurant Matteo had recommended, located in a suitably anonymous location, off a side-street from the large Piazza Navona. We sat on an elevated terrace, shielded by trees and enjoyed a bottle of white wine, when I remembered I had promised to call A. It was early morning in New York, but I knew he was bound to be up anyway, lifting weights, jogging or just studying himself in the mirror.

I excused myself from the table and walked to the side while B was thumbing away on her phone.

"So you found her, but she doesn't want to go home?" A half-shouted into my ear. His reaction was rough, but still understandable.

"She wants to stay a few more days to relax and clear her head. I wouldn't see it as a big deal." This was my attempt at taking some weight off of the situation, after all, this was *all* she was trying to do. Take a little vacation. With other men.

"Is she going crazy, Darryl? Is that what's happening? Because this doesn't sound like a very sane person to me." I had heard this resigned tone in his voice far too often by then and it had become a big worry for the soundness of their marriage. He was slowly giving up and *B* needed to show him he had no reason to.

"She's better now. I think she just needed some distance from the incident. I wouldn't be too concerned at this point."

"It's kind of hard NOT to be concerned when your wife fucks off to another country without telling you."

"I understand that. She does too. But I don't think stressing her to come home when she feels like this is the way forward. You told me to go here and find her and I did that. Now she wants a few more days in the city and I think the easy way is just giving it to her. You're busy anyway."

It was when I said this that I realized *I* really wanted to spend some more time with *B* in Rome. We had a nice chemistry here and I thought I had seen lots of the "old" *B* since the other night. I wished I could have bottled up this good feeling of sanity in case it evaporated when we came home.

"Okay, if this is what she wants, I'll give her the space. I've always been understanding when it comes to her wishes. But I need you to really keep an eye on her, I'm worried she'll do something stupid. I haven't seen her like this before."

"You have my word on that. I'm sure we'll be back in LA in no-time, re-energized and ready for a new start." This wasn't really true, I had no idea what the outcome of this trip might be, but I had to come up with something positive to say.

After I finished the phone call I had a hard time telling whether I should be impressed or scared by how casually *A* dealt with his wife's emotions, wasn't he worried enough to come for her? Why didn't he talk directly to her? And why didn't she talk directly to him? Had things gotten so bad they needed me as a mediator for everything? At that point I didn't know.

When I got back the table I didn't want to tell *B* about my gloomy prediction, I needed to help her maintain her refreshingly good mood.

"So what did he say?" *B* jumped at me like a starving dog.

I sat down and took a sip of sparkling water, "Well, he supports you and whatever you need to do to feel good about yourself again. He says you should take your time and that he loves you very much." I said, with lots of icing on top.

B made a wheezing sound to this. "If he was still passionate about me he'd come here himself and drag me back to him. He's a changed man, Darryl."

"Well, in all fairness, you left him without a word and went to Rome to hang out with another man, friend or whatever. So let's try to see this in a balanced way. I think you have both changed and it's time to either get used to the situation or deal with it. Hiding from each other won't exactly help, although I understand your need for a break."

B's voice traveled up a pitch, "Balanced way? I don't think there's anything balanced about human relationships? Only single people talk like that."

That hurt. It really did. I hated being reminded of how lonely I was, because most of the time I thought I was fine. I decided to take a step back and get us to smoke the peace pipe.

"You might have a point. All I'm saying is that I think he's being an adult in giving you the space you need. Don't take it as an offense. All is good in the hood."

"I don't know which hood you're referring to, but I can't see much good in this situation right now. It's kind of hard to shake the feeling that he's just *over* me and it makes me want to be over him too."

B poked around her food with her fork and looked like a mix between pissed-off and miserable. It made my heart sink.

"Is it that easy to be *over* someone after five years? That sounds ridiculous to me. I think you're just protecting your feelings. There's still plenty of life in your relationship and you know it. But you must both be willing to sit down with each other and blow some life in it."

"You and your metaphors. The heart knows what the heart knows, that's all I can say at this stage. Which in this case means that he's fucking someone else. And I have a strong feeling about this so don't give me some bullshit or try and cover for him. Let's talk about something more fun." *B* finished her glass, put it down on the table and looked me in the eyes. She suddenly seemed changed. Now she had taken on the look of a determined woman, completely in charge of herself and her emotions.

But I feared it was only her acting skills talking.

***

After our late lunch the mood was not exactly down, but solemn and contemplative. *B* seemed to have made up her mind that her husband was a cheating bastard and she wasn't going to let him enter into conversation again. My guess was that she just wanted to put him as far from her mind as possible and although she was smart enough to know that it wasn't going to work in the long run, she felt it was the best decision for enjoying the present, something I couldn't disagree with.

We were walking around the picturesque streets, pointing to beautiful details on the facades and commenting on the remarkably elegant people and on how vibrant and romantic the city felt compared to LA. I noticed how she slowly got more into the groove, a smile sneaking onto her lips and her eyes opening properly. The city had a clear effect on her and I must say I really liked the B that came out. She was natural, charming and humorous. We had a really good time and I couldn't help but think how much we were both smiling and laughing - a rare occurrence those last 12-18 months.

We were standing on a bridge, just looking out on the river Tiber, when I said: "You're like a different person here. You're like that girl I started working for four years ago - the one with the tireless energy and the bubbly laughter. I'm really happy to see that person again."

B wore a quizzical look on her face, "You really think so? I guess I'm more relaxed here, it's the obvious reason. I feel like there's nothing I have to live up to. So what if people recognize me, somehow I'm still not worried the way I am back in the States. I don't need to be constantly on guard and it's such a relief."

"I can understand that, I know you're stressed out most of the time and it sometimes confuses me how anyone can live at that speed. But that's the deal you get with fame."

"I guess it's life. You just have to deal with whatever cards you're dealt, but no matter how lucky you are, sometimes you can't help but feel you got handed really shitty cards. Not that I'm complaining, I know I'm rich and famous and all that and I know some people would gladly cut off body parts to be in my shoes. Still, the grass is always greener on the other side, and sometimes I long for a less complicated existence."

We had talked about this plenty of times and I knew *B* loved her luscious lifestyle and being in the spotlight. But, obviously, when the going got rough, she wanted out.

"That's what everybody feels, everybody thinks there's something over the rainbow, something bigger, better, or just different. But usually small adjustments is everything we need to feel fine again. Like a trip." I smiled at *B*, wanting desperately to keep her mood intact and ride the positive wave she was on. I needed her good self, her *real* self, because it made everything so much easier and so much better.

"Like a trip," she said and smiled back. It was a nice moment between friends that I sometimes think back to. What happened next wasn't as nice.

We started walking again and were soon in a maze of narrow, cobblestone streets with restaurants and their outside tables crammed between the walls. It looked like a setup to attract tourists, not locals. Suddenly a man with a large camera took a few brisk steps toward us, stopped for a second to take a few quick shots, then moved forward again. We had had a nice walk, where it felt like Hollywood and the life we had in LA where not only geographically, but also emotionally far away and suddenly here was *reality*, flashing in our faces. I put my arm around *B* and held up my hand, but the man in the leather jacket and the goatee had no intention of stopping, he had found a target. He got closer and then suddenly, like something swept through my body, I decided to do something I don't think I'd ever done before (or since then for that matter), I stepped up to him and told him to stop it. I stared into his eyes with a wild fire, something I rarely felt, being a calmer, more calculating person. "I warn you!" I shouted in his face, but the man pushed me away to get a clear shot of *B*. This made me see red and I came at him with full force and shoved him to the ground, where he fell hard and his camera smacked heavily against the cold stone. "Let's go," I said to *B*, a mix of determination and shock taking over my voice, and I grabbed her hand as we ran away from the man and further into the maze of narrow streets.

I heard the man shout furiously in Italian behind us, but after a few turns we must have lost him, because a calm set between us. We stopped and looked at each other like we had escaped the jaws of death, when it was only paparazzi - something we dealt with almost daily. *B* looked at me with incredulous eyes and said, "Wow, what happened there, Darryl? You really caught fire!"

"I don't know," I said, still panting from the run, "I just lost it. We were having such a nice time and the last thing I wanted to see was one of those motherfuckers."

B smiled, "I like the way you protected me, it felt like you were saving us from a robber, not a man with a camera and magazine contacts. But you know he might try to charge you with breaking his camera? This is Italy, I don't know how they deal with things here, but you might get in trouble."

"I'll take the risk," I said, feeling a rush of masculine adrenaline and pride. I was happy I'd been able to show a tougher side of myself around her, not only being the eternal, funny friend, but also making it clear that I *did* have her back too.

It was of course not a normal situation for us, *B*

traveling all alone without as much as a bodyguard, but I think we both enjoyed the challenge and the freedom of it. It allowed us to get closer and be somewhat *free*.

"I think we both deserve a glass of wine now," *B* said and we both smiled again.

***

We ended up in a rustic old bar with a marble counter and dark oak features. The place looked 300 years old, but had received good reviews on Tripadvisor and I loved the ambiance. Plus, there weren't many people here, only one or two couples and a lone guy by the bar. I scanned the faces to see if anyone recognized *B* or paid her extra attention, but everyone seemed to be minding their own business. Fame was a weird beast, sometimes you got the over-eager fans who just wouldn't let you go until you called security, but most of the time people were just happy to look, marvel and tell their friends who they had seen. This was the good, acceptable part which I didn't mind. Look - but not touch, was a decent principle to live by.

I ordered two glasses of Brunello and gave *B* a glance. There was a color in her face I hadn't seen in quite a while, a beautiful, soft red nuance that told me that no matter how many paparazzi we might run into, she was still very much "alive" and happy to be here. I was starting to see her reasons more clearly.

"Cheers," I said and lifted my glass. This was the lifting I preferred, wine instead of weights.

B's eyes were glued to her phone though and she had a mysterious little smile on her face.

"Who is it?" I asked, slightly peeved that she was

preoccupied with other things when my mood was so exuberant.

"It's Matteo. He's inviting us to a big party tonight, hosted by one of Rome's biggest art collectors."

I could hear in *B*'s voice that this excited her, which was big for a girl who had been to pretty much any party there was. I, however, had hoped for a relaxed evening just the two us, talking, drinking a glass of wine and enjoying the lack of action. If I had been more in tune with my own feelings and not so focused on *B* all the time, I would probably have realized what was happening inside me. Suddenly I was jealous not to have her for myself.

I couldn't really hide my lack of enthusiasm, "You sure going to a party is a good idea when you're trying to cut down on the drinking?"

"I'm going to cut down on the drinking, yes, but that doesn't mean I'm going to stay home and be boring. I can drink moderately. Don't you think it will be fun?" *B* replied, wineglass in hand.

"I thought the whole point of the trip was to get away from the spotlight?" I offered, desperately.

"I wanted to escape Hollywood and the media machine, not people in general. Isn't it better for me to socialize and forget about the whole thing, than to sit in my room, depressed and think where the fuck my life is going? That doesn't sound very helpful."

I knew she had already decided to go to this party, but I had big second thoughts about her drinking, the presence of Matteo and what other excuses for being uncomfortable I could come up with. It just didn't feel right.

"I have nothing to wear!" *B* said, like she had just discovered world hunger, "we need to go shopping. And it's about time you wore something stylish too, you always look like an accountant."

This was a stab I couldn't have foreseen, I was always classy and tidy, I thought.

"What's wrong with how I dress?"

"Chinos? Seriously? You're younger than me! And they make your ass look big and chunky." Seeing the shocked and slightly sad look on my face, *B* continued: "I'm not trying to offend you, I'm just giving you some well-needed advice. You're single, good-looking and not yet thirty. Bring out your potential!"

"What do you want me to wear then?" I said, with sadness in my voice.

"I have some ideas." *B* smiled, "We'll don you up, it'll be fun!"

And as we headed for the stores, I couldn't disagree more.

***

A man was touching me. Luckily we weren't in a bar, but in a Gucci store and the man was a white-haired, old-school tailor with a pen behind his ear and measuring tape in his hands. I was getting an outfit custom-made, express charge and *B* was paying for it. She was sitting in a chair, watching the spectacle with an amused grin on her face and a glass of bubbly wine in her hand. She seemed to be in a great mood and had already found a 970 dollar black Prada dress she could wear, which according to her was a bargain. When it was my turn, I was so tired from all the walking we had done that day that I was about to faint.

The feeling persisted. My pants ended up being so tight

my testicles were about to explode through the fabric, but *B* gave my outfit two thumbs up and said, "That's more like it! Now we're talking HOT! Hot chocolate!" This bad joke emitted a chuckle from the ridiculously good-looking and well-dressed shopping staff, while I wondered if *B* had had a glass or two too many already. It was going to be a testing night.

"Shake that moneymaker," she said with a grin when I stood in full figure in front of the mirror in my new tight grey jeans-like pants, black and shiny-striped shirt, a teal scarf and pointy brown leather shoes. Saying I was uncomfortable would have been a major understatement, but I had no choice but to take it for one night.

"You look fabulous! Have you lost weight?" *B*'s eyes wandered over my body.

"Yeah, worrying about you is making me skinny," I said in a dry tone.

"But seriously, don't you feel great? This is the kind of clothes you *should* wear! Gone are the days of Grandpa-pants!"

"I feel...tight. But if you're happy, I'm happy and I would be even happier if we could leave soon so we could rest a bit before the party."

We said goodbye to the ecstatic Italian shop crew who had recognized her from the start and was on their very best throughout the shopping "experience". When we were out on the street, *B* slapped me gently on the ass and said, "Now let's buy some champagne."

Sexual harassment in the work place? You bet. Weird thing was, I didn't mind it.

***

I had never tasted better room service food, gloriously prepared by the hotel's Michelin star restaurant, Imago, but *B* seemed far more interested in the bottle of *Moet* we were sharing, which meant I was having a glass and she was drinking the rest. I wanted to drink more, if only to save her from over-consumption, but I didn't really like champagne - to me it was always sour and made my stomach gassy, and I didn't want gas in my new pants - it would blow a hole straight through them.

B's mood was as bubbly as the champagne and her eyes sparkled like the dress she was wearing. In two days she had become a completely different person, which made me happy, but it also concerned me that it was equally easy for her to retreat into her cave of unhappiness again. That was usually how dramatic her shifts were, although they were slightly exaggerated this time.

We were sitting on her magnificent penthouse terrace, enjoying a lukewarm evening and just watching the night skyline of Rome with its lighted domes and beautiful buildings and for a second I wished we could stop time and sit here forever. But we couldn't, because we had a party to go to.

B was in a talkative frame of mind, trying to dissect her issues herself, without letting them color her mood.

"Everybody thinks I've got more to give, I can do more interesting roles, be in bigger and bolder movies, that I can really *act*. Everybody except for the few people who actually have something to say, the directors and moviemakers who rule Hollywood. I don't want to end up shooting these pointless comedies for the rest of my life - I know I'm better than that."

I didn't really like these types of discussions, because it was obvious *B*'s real issue wasn't the roles she weren't getting, it was something else. Still, in a way, she was right. She probably had more talent than people got to witness on screen.

"I don't think they're pointless, lots of people get something meaningful from them, besides just letting them escape their dreary everyday lives for 90 minutes. You're being far too harsh on yourself as usual." I said, trying to kill the topic.

"That's bullshit, Darryl, and you know it. The movies I'm in make as much impact as bubblegum. It doesn't take long to realize they have no flavor, no real substance, and thirty minutes after they're finished, you forget you ever watched them at all."

Since I wasn't a big fan of her movies and she knew this, I couldn't argue, so I tried to find a sub-path on the same subject. "You could always go to Broadway or back to acting school. Maybe look for something independent like Nicole Kidman did with Lars Von Trier? Why not European films? There are tons of possibilities, you just need to be patient. And maybe kick Julianne out, I don't think she sees things the same way."

"You never liked Julianne, I know that. Actually, I don't like her much either, but she's a great agent and my mother's contact and I wouldn't hear the end of it if I fired her."

B did anything to avoid her mother, even if it meant staying with an agent she didn't like. It seemed like a practical approach to her, but just pushing the problem away, to me.

"I'd like to start painting again, you know." *B* said and

eyed me unsurely, probably wondering how I was going to react to such a surprising comment. I knew she used to paint a lot as a little girl, after all she was of the same blood as her artist father, but I had no clue she ever wanted to get back to it. She had never mentioned it before. My immediate thought was that she was seeking his distant approval. Family relationships rarely make sense and we always feel the need to be accepted, even from people who treat us like dirt.

"Well, why not?" I said, in a chipper voice, "If you like it, it might help you to relax and clear your head."

B looked out over the buildings and seemed to ponder my reply. I could tell she wasn't entirely sure what it meant for her or if she was going to start painting or not. It had probably just landed in her head as we sat there.

"I don't know what I would paint though and I'm not sure I would ever want anyone to see my work. It would just be something for me to do to maybe figure things out. You don't really have any hobbies do you, Dar?"

She had hit a weak spot in me, the lack of extra-curricular activities. I was all work and wine, and sometimes in combination. I couldn't help but feel there should be something more, but I had never found something I could devote my heart to. Except for wine and books, maybe. But pretty much everyone drinks wine and reads books so I'm not sure they would qualify as a "hobbies".

"No, I don't. I guess I like reading and talking and wine. You know that wine bar I talked about? Something like that. Or even having my own vineyard would be cool one day."

"Don't you feel like your personality would be stronger if you had hobbies? That you would be more *you*?"

B was now studying me, saying things she had probably thought about for a long time but never said out loud. I was worried that what was coming to me next wasn't going to be good.

"I think my personality is quite clear, I don't think hobbies necessarily have anything to do with your personality. Not having hobbies, is not a statement in itself, I think."

"I mean that you are not so easy to categorize, sometimes I feel like I know you the best in the world and other times I feel like I don't know you at all."

We rarely talked about me and when she said this I had a feeling why, maybe *B* thought there wasn't much to talk about. For a moment this made me very sad. Was I a boring person? I had never heard someone say this about me, but I could still understand her feeling that way, considering everything about me seemed to be about *her*. I had no real life outside the mansion.

"I think the best chance to get to know me, is just to ask more stuff. I'm not so fond of blowing my own trumpet as you know. I work for you so obviously our talks are mostly around you. It's not strange when you think about it." I felt hurt in my voice rise up, but I managed to push it down before it reached the surface.

"I don't mean to be mean, Dar. I'm just saying I really like you and despite us working together for four years, I really don't know that much about you. It's partly my fault, of course. But I also think that, sometimes, you don't let yourself come out. You're so professional all the time."

"I'll try to be less professional then and we'll see how that goes." I tried to smile sincerely, but failed. I wasn't used to criticism and definitely not good at receiving it and her words stung me quite badly. I was having a great time with her and it upset me that my presence wasn't delivering more impact. Whatever that meant.

B was about to say something, but then her phone interrupted her. "He's here," she said and rose from her chair.

***

We headed out to Matteo's car for the evening, which turned out to be a dark blue Maserati parked just outside the hotel. I was suddenly very self-conscious and seeing the handsome Italian with his pinstriped suit and strong jaw, made me feel like an outcast, kind of like a retarded brother *B* unwillingly brought along to her lovely get-togethers for the bold and beautiful. I said hi to Matteo, who nodded at me with a fake smile, then I sat down in the back seat while he opened the door for *B*, who looked absolutely amazing in her black Prada dress. Sitting alone in the back seat didn't make things better. I studied Matteo's pitch black hair with the tiny pathetic locks on the end of the backslick. He was either mafia or a perfect character for middle-age ladies erotic novels. His dress-sense was impeccable and his skin free of blemishes. Besides my obvious and consuming jealousy, there was something else I didn't like about him, but I couldn't put my finger on it. Could he really be gay? Wasn't he too calm, too cool and too intimidating to attract other men? And he seemed far too interested in *B*, but of course everyone went gaga over movie stars. Whatever it was, something about him disturbed me and I promised myself to keep an extra eye on him during the party.

The air-conditioned leather chilled my hand as we drove

off and the smell in the car took a hold of my senses, creating a mix of fresh leather and spicy men's cologne. *B* was talking to Matteo and she sounded like a 15-year old girl who was about to go out on a date with the school hunk. Was it the alcohol or did she really have a crush on the guy? At that time it was impossible to tell, but I hated hearing her like this because I knew it was so far from the *B* I knew and liked.

Matteo said how excited he was that she had decided to grace the party with her presence. He said she had a big following in Italy, something which I took to be a white lie, and how much her love for arts would be satisfied by the collection we were just about to see. I felt slightly nauseous listening to their conversation and realized I was going to have to drink heavily to get through the evening.

After a short drive, we reached a large building that looked more governmental than residential. Matteo stopped the car outside a huge, black iron gate and picked up his iPhone. After a while someone picked up and *voila*, the gate started sliding open. We drove into a large courtyard, parked the car next to a white Bentley and headed out into the crisp evening air. Matteo put his hand on *B*'s back and ushered her towards the entrance, while I walked behind, feeling like a small dog. After climbing a long marble staircase we found ourselves in a huge space and in the middle of a lavish party.

Massive is an apt word to describe both the space, which I would call a loft, and the party. Elegant people were meandering around, carrying champagne glasses and speaking their native tongue in animated and excited tones. Everything was very white, so white you almost had to wear shades to see properly and the walls were lined with massive paintings full of color and strange shapes. It created a contrast that almost hurt your eyes and it didn't take long to figure out that this collector was into the avant-garde, which was something I'd always had a hard time with. But art was the least of my concerns, because I felt like the loneliest guy on the planet, standing there next to *B* and Matteo.

Strange-looking furniture were placed in different areas of the loft, so oddly conceptual you didn't know whether to sit on them, applaud them or throw garbage at them. I snatched a glass of pink champagne from a waiter with a silver tray and drank it in one swift, desperate motion. *B* gave me a strange look, but then her attention was caught by a short and bald man in black. It was Gianluca, the host. He looked like a slimmed-down version of Danny Devito and could compete with yours truly in the white teeth-department.

Gianluca broke out into a huge smile when he saw *B* and came up to cheek-kiss her, which awkwardly had him almost stand on toe, despite her not being much above average female height. He said something in Italian which included the word *bella,* which I knew in some form meant beautiful and then kissed her hand as well. His voice was thick and coarse and it sounded like his vocal chords ground against each other when he spoke and it took an effort to produce a sentence. He shook Matteo's hand casually and told *B* in hampered English that he loved her work, which made her blush. She didn't expect any compliments from artistic people for her chewing gum comedies and somehow she must have thought his comment was genuine. I had a hard time seeing why an art collector would be watching her movies, but maybe he had a secret crush on her or a soft spot somewhere under his black garments that made him extra sensitive to gooey and predictable story-lines? On the other hand, celebrity events always brought out the most outrageous lies, because the rich and famous simply had to compliment the other rich and famous for their glorious careers, even when they hadn't really seen anything of the person's work. It was all a game of *I scratch your back, you scratch mine.*

B hadn't spoken to me in a while so I was surprised when she leaned over and whispered, "Pretty weird place, huh?" after which I smiled and nodded, happy we could agree on something. She wasn't yet a natural in the art world, but I feared this was something she wanted to work on.

After the introduction an insane amount of hand-shaking began. It felt like you were attending a Parkinsons conference. Most of the people were Italian, but I recognized a British guy from some TV-series I couldn't remember and also an American high-society couple who appeared at loads of these events without ever really talking to anyone or making any kind of mark on anything - like wealthy ghosts.

During the mingling *B* gave me pretty much zero attention so at a point I took another glass from one of the waiters and headed over to a corner to "study" the art there. From afar I witnessed people go all silly when they talked to her and in one way I could understand it. She had truly re-kindled her star glow and her body looked amazing in that dress. But she was in Matteo's hands now and our interactions had stopped. A painful reminder that I was more her assistant than her friend.

I turned to the wall and let my eyes wander over a dark painting with a mystical object in the middle of it, looking a bit like a screw or some kind of tool. It was very gloomy and made me even more depressed while I tried to figure out what the artist meant by drawing what could easily be seen as a massive turd in a dark corner.

I threw a glance over my shoulder but I couldn't see *B* anymore. She had probably walked off with Matteo. *Suits her right*, I thought to myself before I took a sip of my wine and let my eyes find the screw painting again. Then I heard a voice from behind.

"Admiring the painting?" said the owner of the voice, a young light-skinned girl with red lipstick and a strong British accent. She was very pretty.

"Well..." I hesitated, "I guess I'm trying to figure out what the hell it is." I realized too late that admitting you don't *get it* at an "artsy" party wasn't a good strategy.

"Don't ask me, I don't understand this stuff at all, I just came here with my boyfriend." She looked at the painting again and added almost as an afterthought or like she was ashamed to admit it, "he's an artist."

I let out a sigh of relief, happy to have been approached by a likeminded person. "So how's being in a relationship with an artist when you don't understand art?"

"I don't think anyone ever *understands* art, we just pretend to and the one who's best at pretending is an expert. Dating an artist is interesting; it all depends on what day Flavio has had - if he's productive and inspired he's quite wonderful and romantic, but when he feels like he's not getting where he wants to on a project, it's not so easy."

"I think that goes for all very ambitious people, on the flip side of the creative coin there's something destructive. Like me, I'm feeling creative, like I could paint something better than that," I pointed to the screw painting, "And yet I feel like destroying it too. Creative and destructive - all in one!" The wine had relaxed me too much and the outspoken, lousy comedian Darryl was out of his straight-jacket.

The girl with the red lipstick laughed politely at my joke.

"You think it's a screw? I thought it was a caterpillar," she said.

"I actually think it's a piece of shit. Literally. Like a turd."

The girl laughed again. I was on a roll. "You should be an art critic," she said and smiled, "You could have your own TV show where you roast famous pieces of art."

I smiled back at her, "That's actually not such a bad idea - Art fart with Darryl Glendale."

This one didn't net more than a grin. "So how come you're here? Since you're obviously not very interested in art yourself."

"I'm a friend of *B*," I said, "and we're here for..." I was about to say vacation, but realized it would sound a bit weird, like why would she do that with a friend and not her husband? "we're here to look at apartments actually. She's thinking of buying a place here in Rome and I'm her second opinion."

Mentioning *B* seemed to lift the girl's spirits even higher. "How exciting! You're definitely doing the right thing, because this is a truly fantastic city. I'm from London myself, but don't see why I would ever move back."

"Yeah, Rome is nice."

"Since you don't seem to like this modern stuff, why not have look in the room where he keeps all the classical pieces?" This caught me by surprise, because I thought this short but pleasant conversation was coming to an end and also because I had no clue there was another art room.

"What's your name by the way?" I said and stretched out my hand, thinking what a shame it was that all good girls were taken.

She shook it firmly and said "Geri" and like she could read my confused look, she added "Like the redhead in Spice Girls, G-E-R-I. Geri."

"Aha, so you're a Spice Girl. I'm Darryl and I'm one of the *Blackstreet boys*," I joked badly, "let's find that other room."

I was happy to have Geri as company, but I knew there was a risk her boyfriend would get angry, which would be an unnecessary complication. But on the other hand, artists weren't so macho and possessive and Geri didn't seem to think it was a big deal to walk around with a complete stranger. Maybe they had one of those "open" relationships?

The classical room was a time machine into the 17th century and most of the paintings in there carried massive gold frames and a sense of legend. The furniture was from the same period, dark wooden and in vivacious shapes and there was a huge golden chandelier hanging from the ceiling. Being a semi-snob, I actually preferred this style from the ultra-contemporary designs that dominated the rest of the gallery. I have always been nostalgic for the "good old days".

I stopped in the middle of the room, stared upwards at what I realized was a wonderfully and meticulously painted ceiling and said "Wow!"

"Dashing," Geri replied, in an accent I thought was reserved for old ladies in hats and pearl necklaces. Despite her young and fresh looks, it suited her. Perhaps we were both snobs.

I saw a painting I recognized and walked up to it, "He has an original Monet?" I said, feeling my mouth open into an awkward shape.

"Of course, this is one of best private collections in the world. He has lots of famous works, Monet, Dali, Caravaggio. It's basically a museum."

"Amazing." I replied.

Geri didn't seem very interested in the paintings though and kept talking, "Did you find anything you like yet? The apartments, I mean, the one she wants to buy."

I don't like lying because it always pushes you further down the rabbit hole, but here I had already taken that step and had to worm myself out of it. I faked interest in the painting in front of me and said in a faraway voice, "Nah, not really, but I'm sure something will turn up." I didn't like how my voice sounded when I lied - all squeaky and shaky - a lie detector would probably be drawing up mountains for me.

"I wonder where she is by the way," I added in an attempt to change the subject and also because I had no idea where *B* was. I was supposed to guard her against the evil who came in suits, long hair and musky colognes, but I wasn't doing a great job.

Geri looked a bit disappointed when I mentioned *B*, "If you want to look for her, that's fine. But I'm sure she's in good hands around Matteo," she said and kept looking at a *Dali*.

"You know him?"

"Well, through Flavio I know pretty much everyone in the upper end of the Roman art scene. I've met him quite a few times, he's a true gentleman."

I was almost about to ask about Matteo's sexual orientation when a tall man in long, slightly frazzled hair, wearing a brown turtleneck sweater appeared from nowhere and started talking to Geri in a sharp Italian tone. She responded in a raised voice, her accent sounding impeccable to my mono-lingual ears and gestured towards me and said, "Flavio, this is Darryl, Darryl, this is my boyfriend Flavio."

Boyfriend? He's your oldfriend, that's what he is! I remember thinking, because the tall and slim man in front of me was at least 25 years her senior. A part of me wanted to reassure myself that it wasn't an uncommon thing these days and another part of me wanted to shout: *Call the cops!*

Flavio shook my hand nonchalantly like he couldn't care less who I was and I could't really blame him either, after all I had "hijacked" his girlfriend. He leaned down like a T-Rex towards Geri's delicate little ear and whispered something, after which she turned to me, said "excuse us," and then the odd-looking couple walked away and left me feeling lonely and miserable. Geri had been a great escape for me, but now she was gone and all I had was an empty glass and some paintings to look at.

I walked around and looked at some more paintings. My head was strangely empty. I looked at my watch and realized time had literally flown and that I needed to get back to *B*. Wherever she was.

Back in the main room people were scattered about talking, and the crowd didn't look as dense as before. My head went back and forth as I paced the space, but *B* was nowhere to be seen and my nervous walking around was starting to attract curious looks from the rest of the partygoers and beads of sweat from my armpits.

Wasn't someone saying something about a roof terrace? That must be where she is! Was the thought that popped into my head after a while.

After asking a waiter I found a door leading to a small staircase in one of the corners of the room. Up there was a glass door leading out to the roof, which was full of plants and furniture and looked more like a lounge. Most of the party had moved up there it seemed and I was soon handed some kind of drink. I saw Gianluca, I saw Flavio and Geri, I saw many of the people I'd met downstairs, but not *B* and not Matteo. Finally I turned to Geri, "Sorry to disturb, but have you seen *B*?"

She shook her head and reached over towards Gianluca and said something in Italian. He looked up at me and said, "I think she left already. Sick." He rubbed his belly to make up for his poor English.

Alarm bells went off in my head. She had already left the party with Matteo, without telling me. How could she have gotten sick again? She wasn't drinking that hard? Or was she? I said thanks to Gianluca and left the terrace in a haste. Once again she had walked out on me without saying anything and I was really angry with her. Was she at Matteo's place or back in her room? I tried calling her, but as usual, she didn't answer her phone. In the end I decided to take a cab back to the hotel, it seemed like the only sensible thing to do at that moment.

But I didn't think straight and just walked out of the building without telling anyone and ended up walking for 20 minutes before I found a taxi willing to stop and take me back to the Hassler. I looked out the window at night-time Rome passing by and yelled at myself for dropping my focus and leaving *B* to her own devices. She was still fragile and could easily be manipulated into anything, especially by an Italian stud.

***

I didn't sleep well that night and woke up with a dry throat. I needed water, but the first thing I reached for was the phone, where I found a message saying: "I'm SO SORRY! I got really sick & Matteo offered me to stay at his place. I hope u got home ok! Love x."

She had spent the night with another man, which in my head could only mean one thing, infidelity, which in another turn could only lead to the dissolution of her marriage, which would make my job situation very shaky. I sighed deeply, walked over to the mini-bar, grabbed a bottle of San Pellegrino, sat down in the sofa chair and felt like a ton of bricks had fallen over me - like everything I fought for was lost. I don't know why I felt it this harshly, it wasn't a typical thing I did, I wasn't a drama queen. After all, I wasn't sure it would cost me my job or bear any grave implications on my personal life. It was too early to know anything. Still, her "betrayal" hurt me more than I could have ever thought.

***

B returned to our hotel just after lunch, chipper and cheerful and constantly on her Blackberry. She didn't say anything about her night with Matteo, only that she must have some kind of stomach bug, because she'd had the same feeling of nausea several times now, with it, timely, reaching new heights during one of the most prestigious red carpet events.

This baffled me. Was she so far detached from reality that she wouldn't even comment on what in my mind was a likely adultery? Wasn't she sorry she abandoned me at a party in a foreign city? And why, if she was sick the night before, wasn't she hungover? Where was all this energy coming from?

Like nothing had happened, she suggested we take a trip to the Vatican, making it sound like the equivalent of popping down to Starbucks for a cream cheese bagel. I said yes, of course. What else could I say?

At that point I thought *B* was completely oblivious (or just didn't give a shit) about how I felt, but in the cab on our way to the Pope's home, she proved to have a better check on her surroundings - she said, "What's up with you today, Darryl? Why aren't you talking to me?"

I told myself to take it easy, but anger burned inside of me and I couldn't help but burst out, "What do you think? You just left me, said nothing, didn't answer my calls and spent the night at his place. I at least thought you could *say* something about it!"

"What are you talking about? I was drunk and slept in his apartment, not in his bed! Not *with* him! He's gay, remember? And I texted you this morning! Since when did you get so sensitive?"

I had opened Pandora's box and figured I might as well dive straight in. I looked at *B* whose lips were quivering with fury and shock and for a second I was going to back down. After all, she seemed to be feeling good about herself for once. But I couldn't help but wonder: at what price?

"Seriously? You didn't do anything? I saw you two. He looked like he wanted to *lick* you! Like some kind of horny cat! You slept at his place and nothing happened and you didn't tell me you left because you felt sick and you couldn't call me because your phone was out of battery? I'm supposed to believe all that? This is not *Gullible's Travels* you know!" A pun like this would normally make me smile, but I was furious. A rare emotion in my body.

"Whoa, what the fuck are you talking about? You think I'm stupid and heartless enough to cheat on my husband? Is this the perception you have of me, that I'm so fucking clueless I don't know what I'm doing? What has gotten into you?"

I didn't know what to reply. Suddenly I felt that maybe she was right, maybe I was imagining the worst? On the other hand, *B* was a skilled actress.

After contemplating my options for a while, I raised my hands above my head in defeat, "Okay, okay, I'm out of line. I just don't know *what* to think, the way you're acting. Can we drop this, please? I'm sorry I got a stupid idea in my head. I was just worried about you."

B put her arm under mine, "You were worrying about me? You're so cute I could pinch your chubby little cheek," she said in a quick shift of emotion, grabbed my cheek violently and tugged it back and forth. It hurt, but I had to be manly enough and pretend not to be bothered by it.

Then she put her hand on my shoulder, "I'm happy we're clear on the cheating thing. I don't cheat, period."

I nodded in agreement, but honestly I didn't really know what to think, because reality was that if she wanted to cheat, I couldn't stop her, so I might as well stop thinking about it. People do what they want. We learn that the hard way.

***

In the square outside of St Peter's Cathedral, the line to the church looked mighty demotivating. I didn't really know why *B* had wanted to come, she wasn't the most devout Christian, but like most celebrities she did get irregular bouts of spirituality which sometimes broke out into a tattoo or God-inspired tweet. All this fame and money must make you battle feelings of guilt from time to time and I guess religion helps you deal with that.

Besides, believing in God is kind of cool. At least for celebrities.

"There's a line?" she said, both surprised and annoyed at the multi-colored cue of people who were there because of faith or guidebooks.

I looked at her with a crooked smile on my face, "Yeah, there are no VIPs as far as God's concerned. Except for the Pope maybe. And the cardinals. And the priests. And...little boys." A bad joke, I know, but I couldn't help it. Besides, I really liked the idea of *B* having to stand in line for once.

"Ha-ha, very funny, Darryl. It just looks so long, that's all."

I looked over at the massive group of people slowly moving forward towards two metal detectors and said, "It's quite fast though, won't take more than ten minutes."

"Ten minutes my ass," *B* snapped back as we placed ourselves at the bottom of the line. I kept my eyes open for people who might recognize her and start trouble, but hopefully standing in line to a church would save us. *B* had also managed to cover herself up pretty well in a big hat and giant Dior sunglasses, and why would a world class celebrity be here, queueing like everybody else?

"I always wanted to see this place, it's on my top five," *B* whispered like we were already in the confessional.

"Which are the other four?" I asked, curious, because I had no clue.

"Since I've been to the Louvre, it's Taj Mahal, The Great Wall of China, Chichen Itza and Petra." *B* rattled off, like it was on top of her mind.

The line moved almost as fast as *B*'s tongue and we were soon at the metal detector. She put her Gucci bag through the miniature car wash machine and watched it disappear. Since we didn't carry any heavy weaponry, no alarm went off and we were allowed inside the church.

Like most people of my generation I tend to believe only what I see, which has severely dampened any interest in religion, but the massive St. Peter's Church took my breath away nonetheless. Just the sheer size of it was, well, amazing.

I looked over at *B* and saw that she had tears in her eyes, "It's so beautiful..." she said, her voice breaking slightly, "I didn't know what to expect, just not this."

"Yeah, it's fantastic," I said, my eyes wandering.

We walked around quietly among scattered groups of people who were either equally taken or just there to say they had been there, the latter being people whose cameras probably experienced more on the vacation than they did. I lost track of *B* for a moment and when I found her again I saw she was sitting on a wooden bench behind one of the massive stone pillars. She was crying. My heart sank down to my stomach because I really hated seeing her emotions get the better of her every single time. I sat down next to her and put my arm around her.

"What's up?"

"I don't know. It just came over me, I started thinking how stupid and immature I've been. I'm 32 years old, I don't want kids, I'm not sure about my marriage and I'm having some kind of career crisis. I'm just so fucked up it's ridiculous and it really, really hurts." She dabbed her tears away with a napkin.

"Don't be so hard on yourself. If you feel like you're not ready to have kids, then you're simply not ready. Maybe you never want to have kids? Who's going to force you? And if you're concerned about your marriage, it's something you both need to work on. Whether it's through counseling or just trying to find that spark or level of communication you used to have again, it's something you have to solve together. Being as talented and successful as you are, there's no reason for you to be feeling like this. You're so much better than that."

B looked up and rubbed her temples with her fingertips, "Sometimes I'm losing hope. Like there's no way we'll patch it up - too much dirty water has passed under the bridge. And saying that you can do what you want with your life is kind of naive, as you're almost always forced through circumstance. I often feel like that, anyway. It's like I'm the ball in a pinball machine, not an actual human being."

I was taken aback by this, was this how bad she saw things? "I think you're exaggerating a bit, we're all victims of circumstance, sure, but that's life. You just need to roll with it and roll with it in a direction you're comfortable with. You can still guide your own fate."

"I know you're right, I'm just saying how I *feel* from time to time. I also know I have lots to be thankful for."

"I guess we're just humans adrift in the giant sea of life," I said in a overly poetic voice to lighten up the situation. We were getting unnecessarily deep and needed a laugh. Which we got.

"You're such a weirdo. And that's why I love you, Dar. Such a fucking weirdo."

She said that at the same time as our eyes met and we both felt it. The moment.

So what happened? Because something happened alright! For an instant I looked into B's shining blue eyes and I felt something. I felt something! Not like an ache or gas or something like that, but something else, something I never thought I'd feel.

Okay, I might as well come out and say it, I felt like kissing her! How the hell did that happen? That would have been the worst thing to come out of anything - overstepping a professional boundary while of course also putting my foot on A's heart.

Imagine what destruction one little kiss can create - a slip of judgment that could haunt you for the rest of your life. One kiss can destroy families, lose jobs and change the lives of many people - possibly ruin them.

One kiss. Think about it.

But how close was it? Did she want me to kiss her? Did I really want to? My mind was buzzing for hours afterwards...

***

The night after *the moment* was strange, anxious and nervous. We both felt awkward and I was increasingly sure she had felt it too, the strong electric current in the air that flowed between us. The taxi ride to the celebrity-prone restaurant we were heading towards, felt long and tense. Luckily, as far as anything lucky can revolve around

Julianne, my phone beeped.

"What's going on? Are you still in Rome?" Julianne shrieked from the other side.

"Yes, we are. Things are okay here. How are you?" I asked, not expecting a reply. I glanced over at *B*, who sat stone-faced next to me.

"I'm dying, Darryl, what do you care?" Julianne coughed, "I actually had an interesting discussion with Paul Berkins, you know the up-and-coming director? He wants to work with her, sounds very interesting. But I can't be sure, he was quite drunk...and flirtatious."

I couldn't believe my ears. To flirt with Julianne you had to be a lot more than *quite* drunk. And I didn't really know what to make of her rambling, she was usually more to the point than this. Maybe *she* was drunk.

"Let's talk about it when we're back in LA, okay?" I had no desire to stay talking to Julianne, despite the tension in the car.

"When *will* you be back? This is getting out of hand. I have so many requests for interviews and appearances I need to reply to asap. Opportunities she can't miss."

"I don't know. She needs time off, she says. What that really means, only she can know. Maybe she'll be ready to go tomorrow, maybe in a month. I'll keep you posted. Ciao."

"But..." and it was my turn to hang up. Believe me, it felt pretty good. And the timing was perfect too, the taxi had stopped and we were outside the restaurant.

We entered through a frosted glass door and came to a sitting room with rustic leather furniture and a fireplace. Two couples were sitting in upholstered chairs, sipping glasses of champagne. They all gave *B* a glance when we entered. They knew who she was, I could tell, not that she wouldn't get looks even if she weren't famous in her nude-colored knitted Missoni with generous cleavage, but they knew.

We were greeted *bona sera* by a middle aged woman in a black shirt and a yellow smile. "Come with me," she said and we followed her down a corridor which led us through another room full of signed celebrity portraits. I thought for a second that *B* must be on that wall, but I didn't ask. If she wasn't there, she would be soon.

Suddenly we were out in a large garden, full of tables with white tablecloths and cosy, dampened lighting. Two well-dressed and impeccably groomed men came up to us, showcasing blinding smiles and expressed two extremely drawn-out *booooonnaaaa seeeeraaas*. We smiled back at them and then a short man with a tanned face and soft, chestnut-colored hair, entered the room and walked up to *B*. They embraced and performed the double cheek-kiss maneuver.

"How are you?" he asked her and looked into her eyes. He had natural, easy-going charm, the perfect restauranteur. "I'm fine," she said, but to my ears it sounded forced and unsure. She wasn't feeling her best, it was all too obvious.

He shook my hand and showed us to a table. We sat down and I smiled at her, "So you're up there on the wall as well?"

B smiled with her eyes elsewhere, "Yes, I'm sure I'm up there somewhere. I at least remember us taking a photo."

"And you say they have great wines here?" I continued. I was nervous too.

"You know I'm not wine expert, but I can promise you they have LOTS of wines."

She was right. The wine list was the size of the phone book and they had everything neatly categorized by region. I don't know if the almost illegible handwritten prices were *meant* to be illegible, but with *B* price was never a problem, so I settled for a 450 euro local wine that sounded interesting. We ordered our starters and fiddled nervously with cutlery and phones for a while. I'd never felt so tense around her and was unsure how to start a conversation, but thankfully she blurted out:

"I need to go to New York, Darryl. I want to work on my marriage. I realize I've been acting ridiculous and selfish."

B's decision-making process was run completely by emotions, so I was used to her changing her mind from one day to the next, but this was still completely unexpected. I thought she was having the time of her life here in Rome and that she was far away from wanting to leave. Not that it's a crazy idea to want to be close to your husband, but I still felt a bit cheated. I was enjoying myself too.

"You sure?"

"Yes, I've been thinking a lot and I'm sure."

I took a sip of wine and let it roll around in my mouth and fill it with happiness. To me, she didn't look one percent sure, in fact, she looked to be in a state of utter confusion. I couldn't tell her this though, because I thought she'd made a mature decision and it wasn't really a decision I could argue with. She wanted to go back to her husband and work on their relationship. Nothing wrong with that, nothing wrong at all. Except for that somewhere inside of me a spark had developed, a spark I had desperately tried to stomp out, but failed to do.

But in the end, it was my job to make sure she was happy and the best way to let her do that was to shut my mouth and leave my feelings aside.

That's how I felt at that point anyway.

"Okay. Sounds sensible to me. I'll call the agency and have them book the first plane out. There should probably be something tomorrow afternoon." I said, trying my best to sound unaffected. But I did feel some kind of lump in my throat.

"Yes, please. Do you think I'm crazy? You give me that look."

"This is very sane. You want to be with your husband, that's great news." I really tried my best, but I couldn't manage to sound convincing.

"You act strange, Darryl. What is it?"

"I kind of like Rome, I guess."

"Well, I do too. I had a great time here, but I *really* need to do this. We can go back soon, do a reunion tour." We both smiled to that, although the smiles had a hint of sadness.

"You know what?" *B* said, changing her tune to something more upbeat, "let's go out tonight. Let's have a fun last night in the city we both love."

I liked the idea. At least one more night before my jolt back to reality. Little did I know what that night had in store.

***

The next day I woke up in bed, naked, a rancid smell of death in my mouth and a throbbing in the back of my skull. I struggled to lean my head over to the side of the bed and saw *B*, sitting on a chair, drinking from a bottle of Perrier and looking at me like I was some kind of circus act.

"How you feelin'?" She asked me, surprisingly chipper in

her voice.

"Like death," I croaked.

"Good. It was worth it though, we had a blast." She had a mysterious little grin on her face.

"Since I don't remember much, it sure blasted my brain," I said and closed my eyes again.

Thoughts which hit me that exact moment: *What happened really? Why am in B's bed? Why the hell am I naked? And why does B have that tilted smile on her face, like she knows something I don't?*

I took the bed linen and covered myself while I walked over to the bathroom, feeling a crunch in my head with every step.

"You don't need to cover yourself," she said and laughed, "I've seen it all."

"What? What do you mean?" My pulse was accelerating.

"Well, when we got home you were quite cuddly. You undressed and wanted to lie close to me and sleep in my bed. And despite being pretty much unconscious you were dry-humping me for a while before you passed out." *B* laughed. She thought it was hilarious. I didn't.

"You're joking?"

"No. There was only one thing alive on you and it was THAT thing." *B*'s eyed travel downwards and fastened on where my groin would be, if it wasn't covered by the bed linen.

"Oh, shit! *B*, I'm so sorry, I don't know what got into me!" Shame flew slam bang into my face like a stray bat.

"Haha, don't worry about it. If I wasn't dead tired or married myself I might have taken you up on the challenge. In another life perhaps." *B* smiled, not understanding that this wasn't only my drunken behavior, but *real* feelings. I, who had thought the so called *moment* had affected her the same way it had me, was apparently just a horny moron.

"I must have been very, very drunk." I said, trying to salvage what sliver of pride was left.

"Yeah, we were both sideways, but it was nice to see you relaxed and outside your super professional box."

"If that's what you want to call it, but please tell me we can just forget about this. I'm seriously ashamed by my behavior." I gave her an honest and sad look.

"Well, you shouldn't be. It was fun and this trip has been really good for me. You're a great traveling partner, you know. When did you say our plane leaves for New York?"

Oh, I almost forgot. New York.

***

B had promised to meet Matteo for lunch, while I took some well-deserved time off the drama-train to roam the picturesque streets of Rome. I wanted to say goodbye to the city in my own little way: drink a delicious *café,* watch beautiful people walk by me in the streets, and enjoy the feeling of age so deep within the city's bones. I also wanted to get myself a new notebook, because I had run out of pages in the one I was using. Writing a diary might not be the manliest thing to do, but without it, I couldn't have told you this story. And I needed it to clear my thoughts.

Heavy rain smattered on the cobblestone as I walked the streets with my sturdy, black hotel umbrella. The rain didn't bother me, instead it had a slow, soothing effect.

I jumped between shops on Via Condotti and the adjoining shopping streets. I drew in the scent from freshly-baked *foccaccia* through my nostrils and I allowed myself a creamy hazelnut gelato and a steamy espresso in a bar. I was refreshed, my senses had come alive and I had let go of B for a while. For a while. Because she was there, somewhere, whispering seductive sentences in the back of my head. I was of course jealous of Matteo being able to capture her glowing attention almost without effort and not happy they were going out for lunch, but I knew there was nothing I could do to stop it. "The night of the hump" had made me understand that I needed to focus on keeping my feelings out of work as much as possible, which meant that for the moment it was better to be alone.

How could I let myself get attracted to my employer? It was the cardinal sin in the assistant's Bible. I knew the answer of course, the fine line between friendship and work had slowly been erased and it had become too easy to slip over to the other, more personal, side. I realized I had to fix this, that I had to detach myself and float back across the line again, take a large marker and make the line as bold as possible, so as never to be crossed again!

Screw the marker, I had to pull some black and yellow police tape across that damn line.

After walking around for a while, I found an inviting-looking bookstore and walked inside.

I passed by the old wooden counter, from where an older lady with unruly hair gave me a suspicious glance before looking down on her newspaper again. The store was beautiful, it could definitely have been a cigar room or a wine bar instead, with wooden shelves of old books reaching up to the ceiling, plush furniture and soft lighting. There was a lush, red velvet sofa placed in the middle of the main room, where I assumed customers could sit down and sample books. There also a section only for thick, bound, leather notebooks. I scanned the shelves and after a while I found one that fit the bill, light-brown, textured leather, cream pages without lines and a silk sewed-on bookmark - it had that good leathery scent, the new-car-smell. It was exactly what I'd been looking for.

I could have stayed there longer, but I was starting to get hungry again and the hangover made me crave a proper Italian pizza. This was a country where it was fun to be hungry because of all the exciting and satisfying options.

I walked up to the old woman at the counter, who didn't look up until I put my notebook in front of her. I don't know if she was deliberately rude or just a complete scatterbrain since people working in (or owning) bookshops, tended to be a little on the special side of things. But then, out of the blue, a smile came to her face when she saw my purchase. Maybe it was outrageously overpriced, I hadn't checked the price on it, or maybe she just appreciated a client with good taste. When she started punching in the amount in her old-fashioned cash register, I wished I had enough knowledge of Italian to at least start a short conversation. Not that Italians were that bad with English, but Italian just sounded sexier and more exotic.

"You're American?" she said, in what sounded almost like a Scottish accent, *Yurr Amerrricen.*

"Yes," I said, surprised, "How did you know?"

And here the Scottish dialect came in full flow, so grave she almost sounded like Shrek, "After working here for 15 years and meeting tourists from pretty much everywhere, I've become quite apt at spotting nationalities. You have the American look."

I wondered what she meant by that, but then again the answer might not have been pleasant, so I said, "You've run this store for 15 years?" instead, my curiosity taking over.

"Nine. Came to Rome on a whim. Blind youth, you know. Fell in love with the city and a man, got married, settled and here I am." She had a weird gap between her front teeth which made her smile kind of goofy-looking.

"I can see how you fall in love in this city." I replied, but like she wasn't listening, she blurted out:

"But of course I've divorced that cheating, no-good, gel-haired *arrrssehole*, by now."

Sensing the conversation might have taken a turn for the negative and I would end up listening to anecdotes about her husband and all the things wrong with (Italian) men, I thanked the lady. But just as I was going to say goodbye, I thought of something, "What recommendation could you give a man on his last day in Rome? Where should I go? What do I need to see? Most of the tourist stuff I've done already."

"There's a nice wine bar just around the corner. Really old place too, 250 years old or something. Buy a pizza, have a glass of wine, enjoy the rain smattering on the pavement outside. That's what I would do. If I wasn't working."

She gave me brief directions and it turned out I had walked past it several times without knowing it was there.

I said thanks and goodbye and left the divorced and bohemian lady alone with her beautiful books.

The rest of the time before the flight I spent eating a delicious multi-cheese pizza, drinking coke (my head was not yet ready for wine) and jotting in my new notebook. I noticed that getting down thoughts and problems on paper didn't eliminate them, but only made the more tangible.

Conclusion: I was in some way or other in love with *B*.

***

We arrived to a lukewarm May evening in New York City. I was so tired it felt like my eyes were about to roll out of their sockets and *B* was nervous and irritated. We hadn't talked much throughout the flight, mostly slept, read and used our digital devices, I had read Hugh Johnson's yearly wine book on my Kindle, she had watched the latest Woody Allen movie on her iPad. She was obviously tense about seeing her husband again, especially since this was kind of a surprise visit and he absolutely despised surprises and disturbances while he was working.

As we were rolling our luggage out of the terminal, I looked over at *B* who was alarmingly quiet. She had a distant look on her face, which I knew was her worrying pose.

"What's up?" I asked her.

"What do you think?" *B* snapped, "Guilt is what's up - I'm up to my throat in it."

With *B*, the emotional roller coaster never took a break. I understood her feelings, but at the same time I was worried that she had finally crossed the line and done something insanely stupid with Matteo. Images of a steamy lunch date in bed flashed in front of my eyes.

"I feel horrible about how I've behaved towards *A*. I don't know why I wanted to surprise him while he's working, he hates surprises." I had of course told her this as soon as she came up with the New York idea, but she didn't listen. And it felt pointless to say *I told you so.*

"So why don't you text him to say we're on the way?" I offered, the obvious solution.

"No, *you* text him. I feel like the first time we really talk should be face to face. I bet he's still angry."

I couldn't grasp her logic, but I'd always had problems with that - it was one of the major ways we were different. I started typing. I was actually worried A would be angry with me as well, since I hadn't been in touch as much as I had promised. Other things had come in the way; like my own feelings. And to be fair, he hadn't tried to contact me either - an obvious sign that something was wrong.

Even though I knew things weren't exactly peachy, A's reply still shocked me: "You're coming here now? Wow. Now is NOT a good time. I need to focus. Please sort out another hotel, I can't have any more drama right now."

When I told B this her jaw looked like it was about to unhinge itself from her face. The feeling of guilt quickly vanished, replaced by anger.

"Is he serious? Is this what our marriage has become?" She asked me.

There were two routes from that point: agreeing with her or playing the middleman. Part of me wanted to urge her on, tell her that her husband was an inconsiderate asshole, and part of me knew it was my duty to balance out the situation. In the end, I decided what was most important right now was keeping B cool.

"You just went to Rome without telling him and then spent a night in another man's apartment, maybe you can call it even?" I said, harshly.

"Whatever," she snorted. "This is exactly why I'm losing hope in our relationship, work always comes before me. Or in this case probably other women."

I couldn't really say anything to A's defense, because work had a tendency to come before anything. Cars second, wife possibly third. But what could I do but call our booking agent and ask her to get us a room in a different hotel?

***

Reputation brings reservations, because we managed to get a nice suite at the Waldorf-Astoria on extremely short notice. The suite came equipped with a huge terrace, overlooking Central Park and two massive bedrooms. On the living room table there was a bottle of champagne, some luxury chocolate and a handwritten note saying: *Whatever you need, just call for it*, signed with a signature and a mobile number from one of the hotel managers. This was usual treatment for *B*, of course, and she stopped smiling about it a long time ago.

Upon entering my room, I looked at the fat and luscious bed and thought I would like to lay down in it and sleep for three days. But *B* was upset and I needed to be on my game, so instead I put down my bag, took a quick shower and headed out on the terrace, where she was already sitting, drinking a glass of Moet Chandon and looking out over the park with a sad look on her face.

"You know what?" *B* said, as I entered her view, "My mother is in town, she just sent me a text that she met Alison at Nobu and Alison told her I'm in New York. Just my luck."

It's funny how she blamed Alison for telling her mother, when all mother Katherine needed to do was to follow *B's* twitter account. Meaning pretty much everybody knew she was in New York.

"Now I'm forced to meet her for lunch. Yippie, lucky me! Life's fucking great." *B* said, in a morose tone.

"That sucks." I said, because I had a feeling "lunch"

would include me. It seemed like *B* never went anywhere without me these days. Not that I usually complained about it.

"Yeah, it does. Can you please join us? I can't deal with her alone, not like this, not after making a fool out of myself." *B* gave me the puppy-eyed look she knew I couldn't say no to.

"Sure. I'll buy some ear plugs."

"You're my rock, Darryl. What would I do without you? Come join me, have a glass of champagne."

She poured me glass while I pondered the question, "What *would* she do without me?"

***

New York-sounds greeted me the morning after. Cars honking, people shouting, the humdrum noise of millions of feet against the pavement. People were on the way somewhere, all the time. I had always liked the city and its magical pulse, but for some reason I thought it was too chaotic for me to live there for extended periods of time. I needed my oasis of quiet sometimes and I doubted I would find it in the Apple.

One thing I would find in New York though was my hacker friend Cesar, and I had arranged for us to meet for dinner, which I looked forward to as a nice break from constantly being around *B*. Don't get me wrong, I still had feelings for her, it was actually the biggest reason I needed a break. It was becoming tiresome to be so emotionally bound to such an emotionally bound person, if you know what I mean.

B was in her bedroom, sleeping with her silk Cavalli

eye-cover shielding her from the morning light. I stood there looking at her for a while, wondering whether I would ever lose the urge to kiss her. It had implanted itself in my brain like a virus and no matter how hard I tried to shake it or numb it, it stuck to me.

Besides thinking about how my feelings changed things, I was also nervous about the lunch with her mother. When they met it was always like opening a can of worms and I don't think anyone of us honestly looked forward to it. But B had never been able to say no to her mother and the easiest thing to do was just to go along with it and pray it would be relatively painless.

This time, my feeling was, it would be far from it.

***

Katherine thought it was stylish to leave people waiting, so B and I had to sit and wait at Nello's for twenty minutes before she showed up in an elegant grey business suit, massive Ferragamo glasses and amber-colored hair. Her face was stretched like plastic film from all her operations and Botox injections and whatever natural features she'd had last time, were now all wiped out. She had become a wax doll gone wrong and an instant feeling of sadness swept over me as soon as she entered the restaurant.

"Hi Doll!" she said, and kissed B on the cheek. Then she took a step back, looked her over and said, "You've gained weight?"

I saw B's face drop and felt so sorry for her that I wanted to throw my water glass in Katherine's face. No superstar status or ego armor could protect you from your mother's harmful comments.

Katherine almost threw her coat on a young male waiter, sat down and then turned to me, "And how are you, Darryl? Handsome as ever with that dark, well-proportioned face. You rarely see a man with a few extra pounds who look that good."

Weight was apparently the topic of the day and it seemed like Katherine had lost most of hers. I couldn't remember being able to see her collarbones as clearly before. She was a victim of the Hollywood ideal, where age could be stopped in its tracks if only you had the money and the mindset to.

"I'm great," I said, unsure if I should take Katherine's remark as a compliment. I had never been slim Jim, but I wasn't really chubby in a bad way. Some people could pull off a few extra pounds and I put myself in that category.

Katherine opened the menu and scanned the choices, while *B* seemed lost in thought, horribly uncomfortable already and probably regretting her decision to come. Katherine looked up from her menu and said, "You know I called your husband the other day and he said you were in Rome? What were you doing there? He told me you had a huge fight after that miserable carpet fiasco."

The introduction had ended and round two of the verbal boxing could start. So far, *B* was taking all the punches.

"Was it so strange that I wanted to take off after what happened? I felt sick, but he still forced me to go to that dreadful event. But of course you won't listen to that, because you always take his side. I'm a grown-up, if I want to go to Rome, I don't need anyone's permission."

"But you're married! You can't just do what you want all the time! You have a status to maintain, a reputation, some dignity. But maybe you don't care about these things?"

Katherine was on fire, it seemed like she had no other interest than verbally attacking her daughter. Like always, I wanted to protect *B*, but here I felt like there was nothing I could do.

"Can you stop being such a fucking bitch? Otherwise, we'll leave." *B* stood up from the table, holding her handbag. She wasn't playing around, she would really *leave*. I noticed one of the waiters looking at us with big eyes.

To my surprise, Katherine raised her hand up in defeat, "Stay. Please stay. I went too far, I know. I've *had a bad day.*"

B looked at her mother for a few seconds before she sat down again and said, "Why have you had a bad day?"

Right about here the food came and gave us a friendly break in the conversation. I dug into my Norwegian salmon ravioli with gusto and for a second I forgot about the lousy mood Katherine brought with her from hell.

"This was excellent," Katherine said, forking down some lobster. The first positive thing she had said all lunch.

"You didn't reply when I asked you why you're in such a bad mood?" *B* said, sounding slightly more relaxed to have the topic changed.

Katherine dabbed her mouth with her napkin and sipped her water anxiously before she replied, "It's a bit complicated with Hugh right now."

Hugh was Katherine's so called *boy*friend, a Hemingway-style business mogul who seemed more than happy to be paying for her luxury lifestyle and countless surgeries. *B* had never met him and with Katherine's track record with men, it was likely she never would. We had googled him though.

"Complicated in what way?" *B* said.

"He's always busy! He gives me his credit card and tells me to go shopping, but then he doesn't spend any time with me. He's always having drinks with his business partners and comes back really late every night. I thought this trip would be about *us*, but we've hardly spent any time together at all. It's like he doesn't want to be with me, yet he's still very affectionate when he's actually around me."

I could see why someone would want to avoid Katherine, but maybe not while dating her?

"He sounds like a very busy man. Are you in love with *him* then? He's apparently richer than a leprechaun," *B* said in a dry tone.

"Don't be rude. I'm not seeing him for the money, we have a really strong connection."

"A really strong connection to his MasterCard," B said and gave me a look. I smiled awkwardly, because somewhere deep down I guess I felt for Katherine and her love troubles. I knew how much love, or the lack of it, could hurt.

B was happy that the talk had gone from her recent misfortunes to her mother's problem with finding love and encouraged more conversation around the topic, "Have you talked to him about this? It seems like strange behavior, after all you've only been seeing each other for a couple of months. And you're both old, a good reason to hold on to each other." B pushed her plate to the side, half-finished. She was suddenly very calorie-aware.

Katherine had this look on her face like she was about to burst out in tears and her lips were trembling, "He just waves it away like I'm talking nonsense. He says it's what women do and then he buys me flowers or a necklace and thinks everything will be alright."

Then the lunch date disaster took a surprisingly positive turn and although they didn't connect on the normal mother-daughter relationship level, they didn't argue and seemed to have a pretty good time talking about work, food, shopping - neutral stuff. I had never seen such a natural conversation between them and hoped it would be the start of a different kind of relationship, one built on respect.

***

"Well, that went better than expected," said a remarkably upbeat *B* on the way back to the hotel. She was talking while tweeting or texting or whatever she did on her Blackberry all the time.

"It sure did. I'm happy you both got along so well. It was kind of shocking."

"Talking about getting along, I'm going out with *A* tonight. We're having a "date". He just texted me."

"Well, that's great news. Seems like things are working out." I said, with all the enthusiasm I could muster.

B chuckled, "You're so goddamn positive I want to punch you in the ribs sometimes. You can't say that things are working out when I haven't even met him yet. He might want to break up."

We walked past a newsstand where I saw the guy stare at *B* like he had just seen a holy spirit. "Look!" I said and pointed at one of the Cosmopolitan covers, where a heavily photoshopped version of her was smiling at us.

"It's out already? That's fast. Buy a copy."

I stepped over to the shocked vendor and started browsing through my wallet for change and from the corner of my eye I saw two guys with massive cameras head towards her. Paparazzi. I took the Cosmo, threw him a five-dollar bill and ran over there just in time to cover the camera crossfire.

"Let's go," I said, holding my hand up to them, "Fuck off guys, get a real job." This was pretty much what everybody said when facing the paparazzi - it came like a reflex. In all honesty, they had a job. Not a very sympathetic one, but at least a job.

"Get one yourself, asshole," said a guy wearing a Fonzie-style leather jacket. Then another one shouted: "*B*, tell us, how's your tummy? Do you have any more throw-ups to give us? Or maybe you have some babies bubbling in there?"

I saw how the baby comment hit *B* like a slap in the face. She took a step towards the guy and spit him in the face. He grinned and shouted "fuck!" but before he had time to react, we ran. And luckily we were not far from the hotel and managed to get inside before the hotel guards held off the paparazzi.

"You okay?" I asked when she sat down on the bed. "Yeah, I'm good," she replied, but her voice was sad and weary. "Let's read the article," she said, motioning for me to join her.

So I sat down and looked at her and thought that I loved her.

***

I was very happy to see Cesar's round and babyish face across the table from me later that night at Chinatown on the Lower East Side. Chinatown was Cesar's favorite restaurant and had an almost magical feel to the decor, making it easy to image you were in a fine dining establishment in China in the 30s. I put a steaming and delicious chicken dumpling in my mouth and looked over at my friend who was sipping his beer with a content little smile on his face.

"You're hot for her, aren't you?" Cesar said, after finishing his sip. His comment almost made me choke on my dumpling, because I hadn't been talking much about *B* at all. But Cesar's levels of perception had always been high.

"What makes you say that?" There was a slight quiver in my voice. I'm a bad, bad actor.

Cesar laughed, "There's something different about you. You sound anxious when you're talking about her. And since you're spending almost all your time with one of finest dames in the world, it would be kind of crazy not to feel *anything* for her." Cesar smiled under his mane of dreadlocks. He wasn't a looker, Cesar, but he had lots of personality. Not always an attractive personality, but at least lots of it.

I lowered my voice, "To tell you truth I never had any romantic feelings whatsoever towards her, until this trip to Rome that is. Then they came over me like a smack on the head and I don't know how to go back to being normal, to feeling neutral. I'm not head over heels in love, it's more like the feeling comes and goes."

"I've told you before that nothing good can come out of being someone's assistant." Cesar finished his beer and looked at me like he had me all figured out. He was sometimes Mr. Know-it-all.

"You never liked my job, LA, or the celebrity world, I know that. But I actually *like* it, I just never thought it would end up like this. It's like I'm a teenager all of a sudden."

Cesar's forehead wrinkled as he put on his serious, contemplative face. Then he brightened up, "You know Britney and her agent got together, seems to be working out just fine."

"I'm not her agent and this is different, *B* is still married, she says she wants to work on it and, we have to be honest here, there's no way in hell she's romantically interested in me, no matter how many compliments she gives me or how much time we spend together. I just need to stop thinking about her like this and start being a professional again."

"I think you make it sound easier than it is. You're in love, man. It's not something you turn on and off like a light switch. In a way, I think this is the best that could ever happen to you. Maybe now you'll realize it's not healthy working the way you do. When did I hear about you seeing a woman or doing something that didn't involve work? You're almost 30, you can't keep dodging real life just because you're too comfortable where you are."

Cesar was harsh and direct, but maybe he was right, maybe this what was I needed to hear. When I started working for the Johnsons, we talked about it and both of us saw it as a short but interesting stint. A stint that had tallied up to more than four years.

"What can I say? I'll think about it. Can we talk about something else now? Like what's up in *your* life? New job and everything."

Cesar grinned like a guy selling men's cologne from a trench coat, "Yeah, mobile game developer - small, funky company, great atmosphere, relaxed guys. I could wear flip-flops to work if I wanted to. It's awesome."

I know Cesar could get away with just about anything because of how good he is. Genius usually generates some kind of carte blanche.

"And women?" I asked, thinking he'd have as little news as I did.

"I've actually met a girl from Toronto. Online, not IRL yet. She's perfect on paper, a real beauty, great personality, similar interests. She's actually coming here for a work interview soon so we'll get to meet properly." Cesar's eyes glowed, something I usually only saw when he worked the hash pipe. He'd probably been single too long. Like me, which made it hurt a little.

"You and your computer abbreviations. What's her name?"

"Rosa."

"Interesting. But I wouldn't set my hopes too high, she haven't even met you yet. You probably sent her a picture of an underwear model instead of your moldy baby head."

"No, when it comes to online dating, I believe in complete honesty. And I know she'll love me. I mean how can you *not* love this beautiful face?" he said and smiled.

We talked, ate and drank and I was feeling relaxed in a way I hadn't in a long time, it was almost like pissing after holding it in for a whole day. I'd been in a dire need of human interaction that didn't involve *B* and when I finally got it, I felt much lighter.

But then, on the walk home from an Irish pub Cesar frequented, she called and I was drawn right back in her web.

"Hey," I said, not sure what to expect.

First all I got was silence, but then her voice jumped inside my right ear, "Where are you? I need to talk."

She always had a need to talk so that was nothing new, but it sounded more urgent than usual.

"Darryl? Darryl? What are you doing?" *B* said, when I failed to reply for 2.5 seconds.

"Sorry, you're breaking off." I lied, "I'm in Midtown, on my way to the hotel, where are you?"

"I'm here, in the room and I need you to take a cab and get your ass over here now."

"Sure, I'll be there as soon as I can." I said and hung up.

***

B needed a shoulder to cry on and I was her shoulder guy. I sat on her bed and listened to her cry and talk and cry some more and although I was obviously distraught by it, I was also so tired I was about to fall asleep.

"He was in a bad mood already when I got there. It was quite late and he was tired and he'd had a drink or three. I only wanted to kiss and make-up, but he was too tense and too annoyed about the Rome thing. He asked me why I did these crazy things, if I had a lover there, how I could keep on embarrassing him. We argued and he started shouting at me, things like *stupid whore!* and *I don't understand how I ever fell for you.* It was horrible!"

She wiped her tears with a hotel towel, while I put my arm around her.

"I said I was confused and needed time alone to think and figure things out and that maybe a move or some kind of change would do us good. You know, to just live somewhere else for a while? But then he went crazy and said: "So you think your problem is LA? Let me tell you what your problem is - you're a nutcase - that's the fucking problem!"

"It went on into the night and it felt like it was over and I was so sad and I told him I don't want a divorce, that I just want things to be good between us again and that I want to feel good about myself too. But then he countered that I only think about myself and we ended by throwing some more nasty remarks at each other before I took a cab back here. I think this is it, Darryl. It's over. It sure didn't feel like he wanted it to go on."

B started crying again. I knew I needed to pull all my strength together to soften this train wreck of a situation and spoke softly, "First I think you need to breathe, because you're freaking me, yourself and the whole hotel out. This is one fight, one out of the hundreds you've had, it doesn't have to mean you're splitting up. You didn't think he'd be overjoyed about Rome did you? This will obviously take some time for you guys to work on."

"But it's not like I threw up on a red carpet and flew to Rome out of nowhere. Our relationship hasn't been good for some time and I'm not the only one to blame for that. And he must know that too."

"I agree. And that's why you have to work together. Give him some time and he'll come around. I wouldn't start discussing your relationship in the middle of the most important movie project of his career. That's why he wanted to stay in separate hotels, remember? I think this so called date might have been a really bad idea."

B's voice was cracking up, but at least she had stopped crying, "I think he wants to stay in different hotels because he's already met someone else. That's what it feels like."

Then there were more tears and seeing them really hurt. I hugged her tight. A crying woman or child broke something inside of me every single time and I wanted so badly to protect her. And for a second I thought *A* actually had found someone else. It would explain a lot.

We held each other for a while before my thirst really was killing me and I had to get some liquid. We were nearing the morning hours and we were both exhausted and sad. "You want something to drink?" I said as I walked over to the mini-bar.

"Yeah, Perrier, please."

As I grabbed two small bottles, I heard her voice from behind, "Maybe he's right in a way, maybe we just aren't great for each other anymore."

B was lying on her bed, looking at the ceiling, tears slowly drying on her face. She just couldn't stop crying. I still thought she was beautiful. "How could anyone want to divorce you? You're so beautiful I get goosebumps just by looking at you." This came from the heart, without any brainpower going through it. It was pure, unfiltered emotion. I guess I'd had it with defending their relationship, maybe this was where I stopped believing in it, I don't know. I was in love with her and part of me hated myself for it.

"I don't know, we don't have as much fun anymore. And we never really liked the same things, as you know. Reality has caught up with us and instead of banging our heads against a wall, trying to find an improbable happiness with each other, maybe we need to take a step back and find it somewhere else?"

"Yeah, maybe. But aren't all couples like that after a while? You always wish you had more in common, more understanding of each other, the passion of being freshly in love - you always want more. But there are a lot of other things to marriage as well - companionship, being there for each other, a more long-term kind of love."

I noticed how my voice went up a pitch. I should probably have stopped after *yeah, maybe,* but I couldn't. I guess because I felt strongly that people were giving up too fast on their relationships these days. I know it makes me sound like I'm old-fashioned, but I'd seen too many break-ups and divorces in Hollywood, relationships where two massive ego's compete, trying to find common ground and fail fast. Why did they get married then? What was the rush? Why were people so crazy about marriage? And why was it such a small thing to break it off?

Marriage was becoming absurdly devalued.

B couldn't help but notice my feelings, "Wow, listen to you! You're such a romantic that not a day goes by without me wondering how you're still single. Are you gay?" It should have been an obvious joke, but she looked a hundred percent serious.

"Would I be dry-humping you if I was?" I gave her a sly smile.

This finally helped to stop her crying, "Yeah, you're right. You're pretty straight. Weird, but straight."

In a moment of emotional inspiration, I sat down next to her on the bed again, grabbed her hand and just held it. We didn't say anything. I understood then that what *B* needed most was a friend, not a lover, and that I had to put my feelings aside, not only for my own sake, but for hers too.

After a little while I felt my eyelids close so I unclasped my hand from hers and said: "You know what? Let me talk to him tomorrow. I'll try to get my head around how he really feels, because if there's one thing I'm sure of it's that he loves you very much and he would fight hard for you to stay together. And if, and this is a big IF, he wants a divorce, I will be here for you to help you through it. No matter what, I'll promise you you'll come out feeling great."

B kissed me on the cheek and whispered in my ear: "You're the best. The best."

And with that slightly positive finish to a bumpy evening, we went to sleep, I in my bed and she in hers.

***

I found myself opposite action hero, *A*, in a smoky gentleman's lounge, holding a tumbler of 21-year-old Scottish single malt whisky. The arm chair was made of old British leather and was so comfortable I could have stayed in it for the rest of my life and probably died a fairly obese, but happy man. *A* was thumbing through a cigar aficionado magazine and looked haggard. Work and marriage combined had stressed him out and the way he was killing the whisky was a clear indication that something was badly wrong. I looked at him and felt a wave of guilt, after all, I was now not only the assistant, but also a guy who was very attracted to his wife.

Not that he knew this of course.

A put the magazine down, scanned the tall bookshelves on the wall and then our eyes met.

"So how was Rome? You had a good time?" he said, his eyes burning.

"It was very nice. Amazing city, fantastic food."

"And wines of course." *A* filled in, his voice wooden and far away.

"Yeah, great wines. Everything was pretty good. Besides *B* being up and down of course, but she seems better now." I don't know what I meant by this, my nerves were talking, not my brain.

"She seems better? When I met her yesterday she didn't *seem* better?" *A* put his glass down with a *clunk*. He was angry.

I had to think fast. "When she left Rome, my impression was that she felt re-energized, but when she came back from your dinner yesterday she was in tears. She said you had attacked her and that you had mentioned separating. She was very upset." I was impressed by my own loyalty here, it was like I was defending *B*, no matter how precarious my own situation was, something which felt both natural and good.

"I didn't attack her. I told her the way she behaves, it's impossible to stay married to her. What kind of wife flies off to another country without telling you? I can bet my left butt cheek she wasn't there to go on a museum tour either."

I knew what *A* implied, but didn't want to get into it, perhaps for egotistical reasons. "She wanted to get away from everything. The whole vomit thing, paparazzi, the lifestyle. I guess it's *kind of* understandable although it wasn't the most mature way to deal with it."

A scoffed, "Getting away from everything meant getting away from me and that's *not* how you deal with stuff when you're married. That's how irrational and insane people behave, people who are better off alone." He raised his finger and looked towards the bar, he wanted a third whisky or whatever number he was on.

"She didn't want to get away from you, she wanted to get away from herself, from her image and the public eye - the Hollywood perception of her."

"The Hollywood perception of her..." *A* mocked my voice,

"What kind of talk is that? What perception? Despite throwing up on national TV, Hollywood loves her! She wants to get away from that? She wants less love? Because in that case I think she's doing a swell job!"

A was channeling all his frustration at me so before he hit me in the face or whatever was going to happen, I felt I better point it out.

"Hey, man, I'm just the messenger here. I'm on your side, well both of your sides. I want you to stay together and I think that whatever issues you might have, they could be worked out. She's going through some kind of existential midlife crisis and we need to help her get through it."

I took a sip of the smokehouse whisky and let it burn the back of my throat. I wasn't enjoying this. Neither the whisky, nor the conversation. I wished I was back in Rome with *B* and a beautiful glass of red.

A raised his hands apologetically, "Sorry, I didn't mean it was your fault in any way, of course not. I'm just so frustrated with her, she's up and down, up and down, like a fucking yo-yo. It's been five years and she's still behaving like a spoiled brat. This time she lost it. I'm trying to be gentle and understanding with her and everything, but it doesn't seem to sink in."

I hadn't seen him like this before, he was edgy and nervous and kept touching his wedding ring with his right hand. Maybe he wondered why it was still there.

"Yes, she hasn't been feeling too good about herself and it's obvious she needs some kind of change. But I know she cares so much about you and that she wants you to be together. And deep down she understands how difficult she's been during this time." I sounded like a politician and I didn't like it, and neither did *A*.

He finished his third glass of whisky and looked at me, "You know what, Darryl. This is not your fault in any way, you've always been a good sport, but to be honest with you I've had it. I want to raise a family and be with someone who's stable and reasonable. No matter how much I love her, the fact is she drives me crazy and I hate being crazy. It doesn't work for me. And that's why I'm filing for divorce."

There it was. *A* had finally given up. I felt my whole body go numb and no matter how hard I tried, I couldn't swallow and I couldn't speak. It shouldn't have come as a huge surprise to me, but it did. It was huge. Things were changing now, changing badly and changing for good. It wasn't like *A* to make a decision and then change his mind, so I was pretty sure there was no turning back. I knew he'd been wanting kids for at least a couple of years now, after all he was turning 40 next year and probably would have wanted one much sooner. Even in his previous relationship, with Dora, the much younger half-Venezuelan model he was seeing for three years, having kids was up for discussion, but instead she suddenly decided she wanted to break up with him. It took him a while to get over that, but when he finally did, he met *B* at the Vanity Fair Oscar's party five years ago, and became enchanted by her natural charm and beauty. Sadly, the spell had lifted and the transition over to a bigger family or at least a more stable marriage hadn't happened. In Hollywood, patience wasn't a product in abundance and *A*'s had run out.

The look on my friend's face passed from anxious to sad and distant. He had started the process of coming to terms with another failed relationship and was dying to move on. At least so it seemed.

"You sure you're not going too fast? You haven't really talked about it," I tried, when I had regained my voice.

"But I have thought a LOT about this, Darryl, and for some time. It's not like I've stopped loving her, it's just that I can't be in a relationship with her. It's not right for either of us, we want too many different things and I've reached the point where I just can't see it working anymore."

I slammed the whisky down my throat and let it burn like the news I'd just received - news which needed their fair share of drink to be digested. I tried to gauge how I felt despite the shock and the only emotion I could find was anger, anger for their sake, in a way for love's sake. I'd like to think every failed relationship made a small scratch in the universe. And it made "true love" seem close to impossible.

"So how's the movie coming," I said, trying to change the subject. I wanted to get out of there the quickest way possible, because I needed to think this out alone before I talked to *B*.

"It's going okay, maybe not really what I had envisioned from the outset to be honest. It's a lot harder than I thought to be a director and this domestic drama hasn't really helped my focus a whole lot."

It sounded like *A* thought his movie not turning out as planned was a bigger loss than his marriage. Maybe he just tried to block out how he really felt. I hoped so.

"How long have you got left to shoot? About a week, right?"

"Yeah, something like that. Might be an extra day or two, depending on a few scenes. And during that time I really need to focus on the movie. Can you make sure I get this space? We have nothing more to say to each other for now and can start dealing with the practical stuff once we're back home." *A*'s voice was so cold it sent a chill down my spine. How long had he been thinking about this? And had he already met someone to cover up the pain?

I left the lounge with a knot in my stomach that would take months to untie.

***

I was sitting in a crowded Starbucks licking cappuccino foam from a plastic spoon. It was a few days after *A* had announced his decision to file for divorce and I was in desperate need of some time alone after nursing *B*'s emotional wounds. She had been crying pretty much constantly and it was the first time since she had learned of his decision that she was actually doing something constructive, which meant shopping the blues away with her friend Alison. Not that the blues were going to pass easily, *B* had a black hole inside of her, a hole I couldn't see being filled in the near future. I had tried my best to cheer her up, but even my usually lame, but uplifting jokes were useless. All I could do for now was hold her and hope that she would finally agree to see a therapist.

Strangely enough, my feelings had gone from attraction to pity, which I was sort of thankful for. It made it slightly easier to deal with what had become a very difficult situation. I hoped that talking to Cesar could bring some light to it and he was about to join me for a late breakfast. And by that I mean he was running 30 minutes late.

While I was stirring my cappuccino and pondering my situation, my phone buzzed. It was Julianne.

"A change of career?" Julianne soon shouted into my ear

via iPhone. She couldn't get her head around what I'd just told her. Her voice was on fire and I imagined her making her hand into a fist so hard blood was dripping out of it. "This is a divorce. In Hollywood that's as big as someone painting their house. Let's move on and not dwell on the past. She needs to step out of her cave and start taking responsibility for her future. For starters she could pick up her goddamn phone."

"It's not that easy. She's very fragile right now and in no state to start working again. She needs therapy and time, not more work." I was too involved in the individual to see the business side of things and Julianne was too involved in business to give a crap about people. This was one reason we never got along.

"What the fuck, Darryl! This is nuts. She can't stop working, not now when things are still looking so good for her, despite her launching food on public carpets. And now that she's single it would be an excellent opportunity to star against someone like Bradley Cooper. We get some romance gossip rumors spinning around, the vomit will be forgotten quickly and things can move on."

Julianne was always looking for ways to spin things. She would have been better off owning a laundromat.

"Like I said, now isn't the time. I'll monitor the situation and get back to you."

We ended the short phone call and I looked around the coffee shop. There was quite a line waiting on their take-away coffees and the tables were all occupied with people reading the newspaper or having a quick morning meeting before rushing off to the office. For a second I imagined myself having a normal job, always wearing a suit, working in a cubicle and spending most of the day juggling e-mails.

It was a nightmare.

My thoughts were interrupted by a familiar sight entering my vision. *How the hell? Could it really be? Was Matteo sitting at one of the tables in the back? And if so, what was he doing there? He was in fashion according to B so maybe it wasn't so weird that he was traveling to New York from time to time, but it was quite a coincidence nonetheless.* I bent my head back towards the Kindle again so he wouldn't see me. Despite my curiosity, I would do just about anything else than to have an awkward conversation with that guy.

Suddenly, I felt a hand on my head. I turned around and saw Cesar with a huge grin on his face. "Darryl smooth-mouth Glendale in a Starbucks drinking a cappuccino all alone, I must say it breaks my heart."

"You're late," I said, slightly shocked at seeing Cesar wearing a shirt, tie and dress pants. What about the flip-flops and casual clothing he was bragging about?

"Sorry about that, woke up late. Good thing I don't have a punch-clock at work." Cesar sat down. "So what's up? You mentioned a divorce?"

"Yeah, things are really going downhill and fast. *A* has made up his mind, papers are being drafted by his attorney and *B* is going bananas. The latest news is that she wants to rent a penthouse in New York and start painting, something she dabbled with as a teenager. I'm actually going out with her and an estate agent later today."

Cesar was far from an expert on relationships, quite the contrary, he never had one as far as I could remember and had instead focused on amassing one of the biggest porn collections known to man. Being a tall, sharp-mouthed, geeky, goofy, weed-smoking computer hacker, simply isn't that attractive to the opposite sex. Still, I valued his intelligence and people-reading skills.

"Seems like there's not much hope for marriage these days. Is there anyone in Hollywood who gets past the five-year-line? Tom Hanks?"

Before I managed to reply I looked up and found Matteo standing in front of us with a big smile on his annoyingly handsome face. He was surely one big "jack-ass in a box". He stretched out his hand and said, "Darryl! (sounded like Daaar-eeel) How *nice* to see you!"

I stood up, shook his hand, forced a smile on my face and asked him: "You're here on business or?" I realize my tone was kind of frosty, but I couldn't help it. I felt jealous and suspicious and many other negative things about him.

"Yes business (*bees knees*). I'm actually having dinner with your boss today."

Dinner? My boss? What was the freak talking about?

"You're having dinner with *B*? Seriously? When did you decide on that?"

"We send texts," There was a pompous grin on Matteo's face I felt like wiping away with my fist. I would also have liked to wipe away my concerns about why *B* hadn't told me any of this. She had been crying for days and now this. Was there something more than friendship after all?

"Okay, well, so I might see you later then," I said, hoping to make it clear that I didn't want *B* to attend any kind of events or dinners alone with Mr. Handsome.

"Yes, maybe. Have a nice day, *Daareeeel*." And Matteo smiled and walked out the door of the coffee shop.

Cesar turned to me with a disgusted look on his face, "Now who the hell was that?"

"*B*'s friend, an Italian guy we met in Rome. I thought he

was coming onto *B*, but it turns out he's gay."

Cesar scoffed, "If that guy is gay, I'm Jimi Hendrix."

"Why do you say that? I mean he takes care of himself like a gay guy. And he's far too attractive to be straight, right?" I could sense the worry in my own voice, because I had never been sure about Matteo.

"All Italian guys *seem* gay, but that's just because they're the metrosexual masters of grooming. You went there for fuck sake - did you think all the attractive men were gay? That would make it Gaytaly, man."

"But that doesn't mean this guy *isn't* gay. They must have gays there, right?"

"Of course they have gays, I'm just saying this guy isn't, okay? I could see it in his eyes."

"You can't see in a person's eyes if they're gay or not!"

"Believe me when I say I have an excellent track record when it comes to *gayspotting* and it's probably because I really like gay men. They pose absolutely no threat when it comes to picking up women," said Cesar with a smirk.

"Well, you don't either, so I don't see how that would help you," I said, jokingly, but I was really in a completely different state of mind. Had *B* been lying all the time? Did she have feelings for Matteo that, in a time of desperation, she felt she could capitalize on now that her marriage was dissolving? I felt slightly nauseous.

One thought led to another and suddenly I burst out: "What would you say we go out for dinner tonight? I owe you one."

"Sounds great to me. Bring your golden expense card, because I'll be starving."

"No problemo," I said, a plan slowly forming in my head.

I was too confused to realize how crappy the plan

actually was.

***

"Guess who I bumped into at Starbucks?" I said as *B* and I stepped into the Mercedes of realtor guy Eddie, who in his Armani suit didn't exactly look like an Eddie, "Your good, gay friend, Matteo. He said you two have dinner plans tonight, well he actually phrased it that he has dinner with my *boss*, meaning you." I was angry and I hoped it came through in my voice.

B was caught off guard at first but soon found her way, "Yes, he texted me yesterday and said that he was in town and suggested dinner. Didn't I tell you? Anyway, I desperately need a break from all this divorce madness and thought it a good idea."

"I wouldn't have forgotten it if you did. Can you be completely honest with me?" I was talking as softly as I could not to have Eddie listening in, but considering how angry I was, it was somewhat of a challenge.

"I'm always honest with you," *B* said, straight-faced.

"Are you having some kind of affair with this guy?"

B's eyes started flashing like she was suffering some kind of epileptic attack, "Oh come on! Can you stop this shit about me having an affair? Even if I did it's not even an affair anymore! I'm getting divorced! Are you trying to make my life even more miserable?"

I realized I had to take a step back, because *B* was too emotional to deal with any kind of pressure at that point. "I just have the feeling something's strange with that guy, I don't like him one bit." I said, weakly hoping she would agree with me.

"You don't know him that's all. He's actually really nice and if you spent more time with him you'd see he's intelligent, cultured and charming. Very much like you, when you act normal."

"Okay, okay," I said, "Where are you going?"

"He booked some new Italian place not far from here. It had a weird name, but I can't remember it. Apparently he's friends with the owner and they'll prepare us something extra special tonight. What are you going to do?"

I couldn't tell her.

***

The first apartment on the viewing list was a duplex penthouse in the TriBeCa area. It cost 32 thousand dollars per month to rent. Yeah, you read it, $32,000.

As Eddie recited the details, talking about the original features like he was reciting poetry; the exposed brick wall, the iPad system controlling all the lights, the 3D LED TV, the marble bathroom with dual shower-heads and so on, I looked around. I couldn't help but be impressed by the warm feeling the apartment gave you, despite being extremely white and lavish on the border of insanity. I knew the amount of light it let in probably appealed more to *B* than all the unnecessary luxuries, because in her confused mind it was becoming equal parts home and art studio.

"You're not going to be lonely living here all alone?" I said, trying to find out what was flying around in that head of hers. The look on her face told me she was already sold.

"Lonely? You're moving in with me, aren't you?" She looked at me like I'd just said the stupidest thing.

"Yeah, well I haven't thought about it. You want me to?" In truth I had thought about it a lot, namely what was going to happen to *B* and I now that lawyers were dissecting her marriage and we had to move out of the beautiful mansion in the Hollywood Hills. Things were changing, big-time.

But like she wasn't hearing me, she kept looking around with an excited sparkle in her eyes. She walked up to the large window with a majestic view over the Statue of Liberty and the ferries and said, "I think this is where I'm going to launch the new me. I can picture it. The easel over here, the paint stuff there, all the light a girl could need and quite a view for inspiration."

"You sure you don't want to see some other places? Get an overview before you make up your mind?" I said in an effort to steer B away from jumping the gun, since I couldn't really trust her rationale at this point in time. Not that the apartment was in any way a bad choice.

"No, this is it, I feel it. Please make sure the paper-people look over the contract before we sign, Darryl. Other than that, it's a done deal."

And with that quick decision we were moving.

***

Cesar's crummy attic apartment was the antithesis to my new abode, but it still worked as the setting for our dinner preparations. And for him to be welcomed in a fine dining establishment his infamous dreadlocks had to go. He was hating me a little bit already.

"I got a job with this hair man, ain't no one complaining about my dreads at work or anything. I've had them for years now, don't force me to do this - this is who I am!"

"Cesar, I promise you this from the bottom of my heart: you will look ten times better without those moldy ribbons. It's a win-win. And it's definitely not *who you are*."

"It's a big fucking *loss*. You know the time it took me to grow these things?"

I laughed at my friend's whimpering little baby face, "That's the most disgusting part of it all, don't you think it would do you good to wash your head for once? You don't need to have pets in your hair - get a cat."

"I'm not doing it, man. I'd do whatever for you, you're my best bud, but I won't do this." Cesar shook his head and I imagined ten thousand lice jumping on the floor. His stubborn resistance forced me to take the rabbit from the hat and disclose the secret to Cesar's heart - money.

"What if I give you five hundred bucks to do it? I'll give it to you in cash today, pay whatever you want at dinner - all this just for cutting that disgusting hair of yours and helping me stalk *B* for one night. It's the best deal of your life."

"Five hundred? To cut my hair?" Cesar seemed to think hard about this, but I already knew what his answer was going to be. Money talks and people listen. Usually.

"Fuck it, D. Fuck it! You need to help me cut them off and then shave the rest, okay? You know that character in the Bible, the guy with the strength in his hair, Samsung?"

"You mean Samson."

"Yeah, Samson. It's like I'm losing my powers, that's how serious this is! But if you feel this strongly about it...500 dollars," Cesar grinned, "is not peanuts."

"Sure, I'll help you cut it. It's a done deal then? Handshake?"

"Deal." Cesar shook my hand and grabbed a huge lock of his hair, brought it to his mouth and kissed it. "Goodbye," he whispered.

It was like Cesar became a new person after the shave and shower, like his whole personality and looks had drastically changed for the better. This could of course have been my imagination or prejudice against people with dreadlocks; because to me it's like this - if a hairstyle has "dread" in it, don't wear it. What kind of dread is that anyway, dread for showers and hygiene?

I looked at Cesar's shiny, shaved head, glistening in the lights from the adjacent skyscrapers and felt a smile creep onto my mouth. When things were up in the air, like they were with *B* and my job and everything, it was a nice feeling to be around a friend who you knew inside out and who you could relax with.

We took two rusty foldable chairs and sat down on the roof of his building. I held a chilled bottle of beer between my fingers and looked out over the city that was so much more than a city, it was an animal alive. The wind was picking up, but Cesar brought two quilts which we wrapped around us as we sat there contemplating what fate might have in store. Cesar was rubbing his head back and forward like he had a hard time believing he actually went through with the haircut, but I guess then he thought about the 500 dollars again and looked more content.

"You must really love this lady. All this just to find out if she's sleeping with that dude." Cesar gave me a look. He couldn't drop the idea that my crush on *B* wasn't going to pass like some kind of fever and at this point I was starting to think he was right. Somehow I had been tainted.

"Well, you shouldn't complain, you look ten times better

already and...500 dollars richer."

Cesar smiled, "Now that it's done it's not so bad. I actually feel fucking sexy like this, like Timberlake when he lost his goldilocks and got his sexy back."

"The little sexy you had, yes, I think you got it back. Cheers."

We clinked our bottles as a toast to a friendship we've been able to sustain despite being fundamentally different in so many ways. I guess we have that thing that money can't buy - just being comfortable around each other. In this day and age that's worth a lot.

We silently watched the sun set before we had to make a move. My gut told me that *B* had probably finished her massage and was in her room, getting ready for dinner. It was therefore time we got ready too. After all, we were going to the same place.

"So how do you know the table you booked is in a place where they can't see us and we still can see them? I don't get that part of the plan?" Cesar was right to be concerned. My strategy had more holes than a golf course.

"I don't really know. I called them, asked them about the best table, they said it was booked and then I chose the one in the other end of the restaurant. According to the images on their website it's quite big so we won't be able to see them directly, but at least we'll have an idea of what's going on. And I bought a wig so they won't recognize me."

"You bought a wig? What the fuck? That's hilarious! You have it here?"

"It's a plan B and I probably won't need it. It's downstairs in my duffel bag with the rest of my clothes for tonight."

"I need to see this!" Cesar was remarkably quick down

the stairs and in less than a minute he was back wearing the medium-sized afro wig I had bought at a fancy costume shop in the Meatpacking district. He looked absolutely ridiculous.

"You bought this fucking thing to wear at a nice restaurant?" Cesar put both hands to his stomach because he was laughing so hard his intestines were about to come through his mouth. "This is the silliest thing I've ever seen! Now you try it!"

He removed the medium-sized afro and put it on my head. Then he adjusted it, took a step back and started laughing again, now with a finger pointed at my face. "Ha-ha-ha! It looks like you have an electrocuted hamster on your head."

"Ha-ha," I mock-laughed, "Thanks for filling me with confidence."

"Well, if you bought it not to draw attention to yourself, I think you're in for a rude awakening."

I removed the wig, looked at my watch and said: "At least it doesn't itch. I'm going to take a shower now and get dressed. When I'm ready I hope you've stopped laughing and started taking this more seriously."

"I cannot promise to be serious if you wear that wig, but I'll do my best," Cesar chuckled.

I put my beer down on the concrete floor, rose from my chair and said: "You think you're such a wise guy without that stinky hair, huh? Just you wait and see what wig I bought for you!"

And with that false threat, I went to take a shower. ***

The restaurant was rustic with a modern touch, but suffered from horrible lighting due to bright red ceiling lamps hanging so low you were almost looking at them while you were talking across the table. I don't know if it was intentional, because it seemed likely that the place had gotten its style by some hyped-up interior designer who didn't see the place as somewhere you ate, but more like a statement. What that statement was, was hard to say, but they had used an awful amount of red, which instantly got on my nerves.

I looked over at my bald date for the evening and told him how elegant he was in his white shirt and black tie.

"Thanks, I haven't felt this tidy since graduation, during which I was probably high and smelled of mushrooms."

"Yes, but the mushrooms we're having tonight are not for smoking," I said as I scanned the wine list. There was plenty of choice, not as much as in Rome, but plenty.

"Stop being such a snob and pick a bottle."

"I'm not going to ruin my meal because you're eager to drink whatever's in front of you. Order a beer or something."

After making my mind up on the wine, I let me eyes search the room. We were alone except for an elderly quartet who were talking so loudly you would assume they had all decided to skip the hearing aids for the night.

Cesar arched his shoulders and adjusted his shirt collar like it was annoying the crap out of him, "This is like wearing a strait jacket. But I guess seeing you in that silly hair piece is going to make up for it."

"Remember that we're here to see if our friend Matteo is wearing a *straight*-jacket, nothing else. And besides, I saw you in a tie the other day, you didn't look that uncomfortable?"

"Look who's all nervous and making bad jokes. It

depends on what shirt it is and I much prefer the clip-on ties from this homicidal silk wire around my neck. Now what do we have to eat?" Cesar opened the menu and made a sour face, "Behold these prices! Seriously? What do they serve here, edible diamonds?"

"What are you complaining about? You're not paying for anything. This does." I held up my gleaming golden expense card and spun it around between my fingers.

"So what now? We just eat, drink and wait?"

"You don't need to do anything really. Just pretend like you're out to a regular dinner. And watch that front door like a hawk."

"Yeah, I always do that when I go out. I'm working part-time as a spy," Cesar snorted.

We ordered a full course meal: starters, mains and desserts. The service was flawless and the food and wine arrived promptly.

"This pasta is great," Cesar said, not obeying any fancy dining principles and practically wolfing it down, making the tomato sauce splatter on his white shirt, "but it's not worth the money, I'm pretty sure I could make this at home."

"Are you serious? You don't even know how to boil water."

"Hey! That's not true - I boil kick-ass water, perfect temperature and everything. I made some herbal tea the other day, tasted a bit like sewage to be honest, but that's the tea, not my water-boiling skills."

"Everything's herbal with you," I said and laughed and at the same time caught *B* and her "date" walking through the doors. She looked stunning in an orange dress, snake-skin clutch bag and black gladiator shoes. Her hair was shimmering like diamonds and Cesar must have noticed my gaze because he kicked me in the knee.

"Ouch," I whined, "Why did you do that for?"

"You were about to salivate on the table, man. Are you trying to be the worst stalker of all time?"

I shut up and ate. Besides suffering from an unhealthy crush on a woman so far out of my league she was orbiting in another galaxy, I was worried about the high-risk game she was playing - what if someone snapped a photo and uploaded it to the Internet or sold it to a sleazy gossip mag? It was too easy to picture the headlines and it would definitely complicate the upcoming paper fights between her and her husband a great deal.

The couple were seated exactly where I had predicted and they couldn't see us, but the problem I had underestimated was of course that neither could we see them.

"I have an idea," said Cesar, like he was reading my mind. "I'll go out and smoke from time to time and on my way out I'll be able to catch a glance, see if they're up to some hanky-panky stuff. I'm sure the Italian bastard won't recognize me without my hair and no matter how strange it sounds, I've never met the love of your life before."

"Can you stop that talk? It's more complicated than that."

Cesar burst out into a brief song, *"That's amore..."*

"Scchhhhh! Keep your voice down!" I snapped.

"They can't hear us from over there. Relax a bit, will you? You've had like three glasses of wine and you're still tighter than a constipated banker." Cesar gave me a prying look, "What exactly are you hoping to gain from this, man? Let's say they're up to no good, what are you going to do about it? Lie down and cry because the woman of your dreams fell for Spaghetti Banderas?"

Cesar was right. So what if she had feelings for Matteo and they *were* having an affair? What could I do about it? Run off to A and sell her down the river? Or just let things fall apart by themselves? Or quit because I can't work alongside my broken heart? I realized I had no plan, I just had to *know.*

"I don't know, it matters to me, that's all. We'll see what happens."

"That we'll do," said Cesar and sipped his beer.

Sadly, I soon understood how flawed my seating plan for the evening was. It struck me cold when I was about to put a truffle in my mouth and saw *B* heading our way. I quickly looked behind me to see why - the ominous restroom sign. It seemed like I couldn't have picked a worse location for our restaurant stakeout. Cesar was on the phone with Rosa outside the restaurant so I was completely out in the open, ready to be spotted and embarrassed. Lacking a better plan, I hastily reached into my bag and put the wig on. Then I started thumbing on my mobile and pretended to be writing a text. I could feel her eyes pass over me as she walked by and I silently prayed that what she saw wasn't her assistant with a dead hamster on his head.

But nothing happened. She just *click-clock* walked inside the ladies' room and I immediately let out a gust of air. *Phew,* I thought to myself, *the wig worked! I'm a genius!*

But I was too early in congratulating myself because approximately one minute later my phone buzzed with a message. My first thought was that it was Cesar from the outside, understanding the danger of the situation or something, but the message header told me it wasn't, it was

B.

"Where r u?" the message said.

I instantly got all hot and cold at the same time, like half of my body were in the Sahara and the other half in the Arctic Circle. Chilly sweats. Why did she text me from the bathroom? I decided to play it cool:

"I'm out having a few beers with Cesar. How's dinner?" I clicked send.

The reply flew through the air and into my heart like a digital dagger.

"Are you possibly wearing a silly wig?"

Oh God, she knows! Sweat poured out of me. This was bad, very bad.

I decided to try one last shot at innocence. "No :) Whyr u adking?" my finger nervously mistyped before I corrected it and sent it.

Then *B* came out from the restroom and sat down opposite me with an angry glare. Suddenly I felt the wig itching. *Itching like a muthafucka.*

"Now can you tell me what the fuck this is about, Darryl?"

If you didn't think black people could blush, let me tell you...we can.

***

After getting told I'm a worthless, no-good, distrusting leech, which ended with *B* returning to her table furious and leaving me feeling as small as a pebble, I quickly paid the bill and left the fancy restaurant together with Cesar. He suggested a bar, while I thought jumping from the Brooklyn Bridge was a more apt solution to my problem.

"I think this is it," I said, my voice cracking, "My employment is over, *B* will start a relationship with Matteo, *A* will hate me for not telling him about the sneaky Italian dude, which will definitely screw up my chances of another Hollywood job and I will be thrown out into the real world where there are no golden expense cards, no LA mansion and no red carpet events. What do I have left? Nothing!"

"This impression of a baby you're doing is really great, but please stop." Cesar said and took a huge draw on a cigarette, "Okay, your plan was pretty fucked up, but you shouldn't assume complete defeat, not with your almost impeccable track record of serving her every need. So you might still have your job and your gold card, but the question that's buzzing around in my shaved head like a giant bumblebee is if this pampered existence does more bad than good for you. It would probably be healthy to have your own place and your own credit card for a while."

He was right. I'd become far too comfortable living someone else's life and when I had started to mismanage my feelings around her, it was even clearer to me that I needed some kind of drastic change.

My friend rubbed his recently bald head for something like the fiftieth time and said, "Why not get your chunky butt out of that padded chair of yours and look for a job in New York? You can move in with me until you find a flat. See this as a chance to break free and stop sulking."

"I'm not saying it's a bad idea, but I'm not sure what I would do. I can't afford opening up my own place yet, at least not the way I want it to be and I don't feel like going back to a regular job either." We were walking uptown and I was starting to think a beer wouldn't be half-bad. A last one before I hit the hay and hopefully dreamt all my troubles away.

Cesar put his right arm around me, "You're probably the smartest guy I know so I would be very surprised if you end up living in a cardboard box or move back in with your parents! You can do whatever you put your mind to; you just need to figure out where to put it."

And as he gave me this compliment, we stopped outside the bar Cesar had intended for us. He motioned to me to head inside.

The place was called "New beginnings". I shook my head, chuckled and opened the door.

***

I don't know how I got into bed, but I woke up a few hours later with *B* breathing in my ear. She was lying next to me for some reason, hot like a desert sun (I'm talking temperature here) and cramping my space. I picked up my mobile from the nightstand and found out it was seven in the morning. I wasn't feeling as bad as I thought I would, the buzz of "new beginnings" were still vibrating inside of me and it felt pretty relieving.

Still, having *B* so close to me stirred emotions I had promised myself to block out. Why was she in my bed? After the storm of hatred she had thrown at me yesterday, it was very confusing. Had she tried to suffocate me with her pillow and fallen asleep while doing so or had she changed her mind completely?

I watched her snoring for a little while, her face smudged with make-up and her hair smelling of cigarette smoke and hair care products. I slowly got out of bed and tucked her in. I guess I would get an answer to why she was there when she woke up, but until then I needed some time for myself.

After a hot shower, I got out and walked two blocks to the nearest Starbucks, where I ordered a large cappuccino and a flavored sparkling water to go. I was feeling a spring in my step as I wandered the remarkably quiet morning streets. I thought of what Cesar and I had talked about and on this crisp spring morning it all made sense to me. It was time for *Ch-ch-ch-changes!* I hummed the classic Bowie song to myself and felt...slightly relaxed.

I found a small park with an empty bench and took a seat, probably with a silly little smile on my face, because despite everything, I was feeling *gooooood.* An elegant woman with abnormally long and skinny legs beautifully displayed in a mid-length skirt and tugging a small white terrier on a leash, stopped not far from where I was sitting. She looked like the kind of woman who does everything with class and never takes no for answer, the kind of woman who rules the world and could make any man feel exactly like that little terrier with just the snap of a finger. It's an attractive look, someone so seemingly in control of herself and her surroundings and I couldn't help but look at her. While I did, the fuzzy little dog sat down and took a shit on the ground with a content look on his face. I noticed it was looking right at me while doing so, almost like it was thinking: *Yeah, right. I'm shitting right here on the ground and this elegant lady, which they call my "master", will have to pick it up. Ha-ha! Like humans rule the world...*

...And the dog was right of course. When it had finished defecating, the elegant long-legged lady took out one of those small, black plastic bags from her jacket and picked up the turd. And in a way the action reminded me a bit of what my job had been a lot of the time, *B* shat on the floor and I picked it up. It wasn't weird that I was getting tired of it, because let's be honest here, even beautiful and famous people's shit smell.

In retrospect, I think I needed to force myself to see my job and *B* in a different light to be able to let go. I had been saving her ass from loads of mini-disasters over the years and gone beyond my call of duty to make sure she was happy. Like that time when she let out a loud fart at a reception and I claimed it was mine or when she was about to cut her hair depressingly short and I talked her out of it thanks to carefully collected images of women who went short and ugly, or all the arguments between her and *A* I'd managed to mediate away from bigger blow-ups. I'd been putting up quite a performance over the years, and although it had been fun and somewhat rewarding and all that, I hadn't given much thought to my own life. I'd been completely captivated by the celebrity glow, the lifestyle, the expense card and that *something* she had which you couldn't really put a name on. That something that, no matter how difficult she was at times, made it seem worth it almost every single one of those times.

But with her marriage collapsing, *B* on the brink of breakdown and the strong possibility of another man lurking in the wings, it wasn't hard to see that quitting my job would be a logical option. How to practically go about it was a completely different story and something that churned around inside my brain when my phone interrupted me.

I was very surprised to hear Jorge, the estate chef, on the other line. Especially since he had never ever called me before.

"Jorge! Long time! How are you?"

Jorge's deep, booming voice made my iPhone vibrate and images of James Earl Jones pop into my head, "Sorry if I'm calling at a bad time, Darryl. But I really need to talk to you. You're in New York, right?"

"No problem. Yes, I'm in New York. We all are. It's been a crazy week. What's up?"

"It's my son again. He's gone off to New York to audition for American Idol. I told him not to, but as usual he ignored my advice and he is staying with my brother in the Bronx this week. I know this is a lot to ask, but I would really appreciate if you could meet up with him and talk him out of it."

Now this is a twist I couldn't have foreseen, "Talk him out of it? Why?"

"You know how those blooper reels are, they'll make laughing stock out of him and it will break my heart. I can't just stand by and watch my son get hurt on national TV. But he doesn't listen to me, he thinks I don't understand what he's trying to do. And that's why I would be very, very grateful if *you* could talk to him."

If I had been in a more sound state of mind, with less thoughts flying around my head like papers in the wind, I'd probably said no, but hearing Jorge's desperate voice made me feel there was really no way I could turn him down. I guess I have always had this strong need to be needed and maybe that was why I ended up like an assistant.

"I don't really see what I could contribute though, why would he listen to me? I don't know anything about the music industry." I said, hoping the conversation would end there.

"Well, I've told him I know someone who works in the

business and could listen to his stuff. I thought you could be that person and let him down nicely. I'm sorry if I put you in an awkward position, but I didn't know what to do. He's my son, my everything and I can't have something happen to him that will hurt his self-esteem for life."

"So you want me to pretend like I'm some kind of music mogul and tell him not to audition for American Idol?"

"Something like that, yes." Jorge's massive voice was down to a whisper.

"And you're sure he would listen to me? Because it sounds to me like he's made up his mind and won't take no for answer, even from a fake record label executive or whatever I'm supposed to act like. What if he just thinks I'm a dick and decides to go ahead and do it anyway?"

Jorge seemed to ponder this, "I know my son pretty well and I know he won't listen much to me, not these days anyway, but he usually takes outside people to heart, especially if they're experienced. It's definitely worth a try."

This was something alright. Here I had walked the streets, thinking that my days of weird assignments were coming to a close and suddenly I needed to don a suit and play a record label exec for a 19-year-old kid who thought he had talent. Life works in mysterious ways.

"Okay, I'll do it," I said at last, "When do I need to meet him?"

Jorge was quiet again. He was obviously embarrassed to ask, which I thought was a nice personal trait. *B* was never embarrassed to ask me anything, but of course she paid for it.

"The whole thing goes down next week, so the sooner the better. All I want is a chance to protect my son's feelings."

How do you argue with that? How do you say no to a

father with a bleeding heart?

"Give him my number and tell him we can meet at Bar Pitti in the West Village at 5 pm today. I don't have much time, so I better take care of it straight away. I'll try my best to play the part, but I can't promise you anything."

"I know I could rely on you, Darryl."

I imagined Jorge smiling on the other end of our conversation. On my end? Not even a grin.

***

My day had done what it sometimes did, turned on a dime. Suddenly I needed to rehearse a plan to imitate a record executive. What first came to my mind was that *B* knew a big fish at one of the major labels. His name was Barry Waldruff and I had said hi to him twice at parties. *B* had told me he had a crush on her and I thought that maybe I could have used that angle to get a meeting with him. But I didn't have the time and I wasn't sure that kind of expertise was needed to fool a teenager with stars in his eyes. I just had to look serious, talk serious and pretend to know what I was talking about. I had done that before.

A text message from Julianne popped up on my iPhone. It read: "OK magazine cover. WHO'S THAT GUY?"

OK magazine? What kind of rotting corpse could they have dug up now? I thought to myself. The upcoming divorce should have been well-kept under wraps, so anything along those lines seemed unlikely. I opened up my phone browser and typed in okmagazine.com.

What met me on the first page was exactly the same thing which met my eyes the night before - an image of *B* and Matteo eating together. The photo was slightly blurry, taken from the outside and through the glass with some super lens, but you could see them alright. I got a jolt in my stomach and an unpleasant tingling saying: *I knew something like this would happen.* I clicked the post and found more pictures of them eating, smiling towards each other, and exiting the restaurant with dreamy looks on their faces. They looked like a couple in love and I hated seeing it. *What was she thinking?*

The article wondered pretty much the same. It talked about an affair and the possibility of a divorce. It was guesswork, not journalism, but was bound to blow up to become *the truth* very soon. I knew the retaliation from A would be swift and that things could get nasty fast. As I slalomed the streets downtown I came to the conclusion that things had finally gone beyond saving. I needed to talk to *B* and tell her about the article and about how I felt, I needed to set things straight.

But she didn't pick up the phone, so while I waited I decided to ask Cesar for help in fooling a lost teenager.

***

Cesar saw no problem in tagging along with my so called "prank", but of course he'd always liked practical jokes, which was kind of how he saw this "assignment" from Jorge. He had even been kind enough to borrow me his second suit, an ill-fitting grey apparition with a no-name brand. It was too tight and it looked like it had been hanging in Cesar's closet since he got his first dreadlock, but I had no time nor desire to head back to my hotel room and bump into *B* or possibly even Matteo, so I said I could live with it.

"So what should we do? Good cop, bad cop? Or we both try to be as gentle with him as possible?" Cesar was "working" from that day (another perk of his new job) and was definitely more into this than any kind of work task he was supposed to do. He had realized my life could provide plenty of entertainment.

"I'll help you with that," I said and helped him tie a classic Windsor knot. He was looking pretty dapper for a guy who a few days before could have been mistaken for a Rastafarian albino baby.

"I'm getting more and more handsome by the day!" Cesar exclaimed as he was eyeing his new, polished look in the mirror. "What was I doing to myself before? I could have been on that show - How Do I Look."

"Yeah, I should have tried to get you on it. And the first thing they would have thrown away are those jeans you just stepped out of. Aren't those the same goddamn ugly ones you had at university?"

"Don't be mean now. I know your heart is breaking and all, but those are my favorite pants dude, my lucky pants."

"How can they be lucky pants when you never got lucky *in* them?" I said, looking at the washed out heap of holes and stains, but Cesar didn't reply, he was too busy studying his features. Without the massive locks of hair, you could actually see them. He was right that I wasn't in my best mood, those pictures of *B* and Matteo were still at the center of my being, but I tried my best to focus on the task at hand.

"Where are we meeting the kid? I'm hungry."

"Bar Pitti."

"They got some great sandwiches there." Cesar said and adjusted his tie one more time, then he turned to me and gave me a serious look, "So what's the news on your love? You told me the cameras caught her last night?"

"Well, the news is that it's news and it looks pretty bad. It's all over the Internet."

"I know it might hurt, but doesn't that make it easier for you to move on? Let's face it, she doesn't seem to be a person you *want* to be in love with."

I didn't know what to tell Cesar. You didn't choose who to fall in love with, you just fell. A part of me of course wanted to move on, let go of *B* and her crazy life, and one part couldn't because I cared for her too much.

I was in limbo.

"You know what?" Cesar said, sensing I was in no mood to talk about it, "let's make some peanut butter and jelly sandwiches to start our appetites."

Cesar snobby? *Fuhgeddaboutit.*

***

We were at an outside table at Bar Pitti, the sun was shining and it was too hot to wear a suit. I didn't feel like taking my jacket off though, because I had collected two onion ring-sized sweat stains under the armpits of my light blue shirt, so I left it on. I prayed that everything would go smooth and fast so I could go back to pondering my bleak future.

"Can that be the guy?" I turned around and saw a Latino-looking guy in big jeans, white t-shirt and some kind of puffy west. As a matching touch he wore a few gold chains around his neck, a Jay-Z style Knicks cap, a black leather Adidas shoulder bag and fake diamond studs in his ears. I couldn't spot any tattoos, but I'm sure they were there somewhere.

But just when I was going to walk up and reach out my hand, the guy strode past the restaurant with confident steps.

"I could have sworn that was him," I said to Cesar.

"Just because you wear gold chains and a Knicks cap doesn't mean you're a rapper. You're quite stereotyping for a black dude, Darryl."

"Shut your hole, albino boy," I said and looked at the crowd passing by our table. It was five to five, which meant the guy was soon going to be late and there was no fashionable way to be late when you were trying to score a record deal.

After two more minutes of nervous waiting, a tidy-looking guy in a white shirt and a navy pullover came up to Cesar and asked whether we had a meeting with Luís. The guy looked more like an Ivy League college boy than a rapper, so I thought maybe it was one of Luís friends, the "Carlton" of his entourage. But I of course stereotyped wrongly again, because the elegant young man with short hair and glasses was indeed Jorge's son. This raised my hopes when it came to relating to the guy.

The confident Cesar took the lead, "We sure are. And you must be Luís," he said. They shook hands. Luís sat down opposite us and put his leather laptop bag on the wooden table. "Eatin' or drinkin'?" he said.

"Drinking, but order some food if you want, it's on us." Cesar said, like he's been playing this part all his life *and* was paying.

"Sweeeet," Luis said and scanned the menu.

"So you're quite a musician I hear?" I said, trying to sound in control.

"Artist."

"Artist. What music do you make? Did you bring a sample?"

"I'm in R&B, hip-hop, I sing, rap and dance. I got you some songs to check out."

Luís unclasped his brown bag and brought out an iPad, which he started clicking around on, "I made this video with a friend of mine, he's an independent film producer, B-reel. I hope you dig it." He handed us the gold-black headphones he was wearing around his neck and the iPad.

"Order two beers and I'll listen first, okay?" Cesar said to me and put on the headphones.

I waved to the waiter, ordered two Heineken and looked at Luís who replied: "I'll have the Toscano panini and a fresh grapefruit juice."

"You don't want a beer?" I asked him.

"I'm 19, dude. I ain't breaking no law."

I chuckled nervously. I completely forgot we were dealing with an underage person.

"What's the name of the song?" I looked over at Cesar who was in deep concentration, like he was trying to count the pixels on the screen or something. He should have been an actor, not a computer programmer.

"Bornastar. It's about the feeling that you just know, you know?"

"Know what?"

"That you're destined for greater things. That God has put some bigger plan in your hands."

Yeez! I don't remember ever feeling this good about myself, especially not when I was 19 years old, but my second reaction was that Luís might have just the right amount of arrogance to go places.

While Cesar was listening to the song, my phone rang again. It had been one of those days with endless requests for communication. Not a single one of them uplifting.

"Hello?" I said as I rose from our table.

"Did you know about this?" I didn't recognize the voice at first, but it soon hit me - it was *A* and he didn't sound happy.

"What do you mean?" I said as a reflex, while I walked a few steps away from the table in an effort to find a quiet spot on the street.

"Don't bullshit me, Darryl. You know what I'm talking about. The Italian guy she went to dinner with last night. I've been wanting to ask her about it, but she's not picking up the fucking phone!"

When I said he didn't sound happy, I meant he sounded furious.

The first question that came to my head was whether I should try to save her ass? Did she really deserve it? In the end I thought: yes. "He's a friend of hers and he's actually both gay and harmless. I met him in Rome." *Why do you worry anyway?* I thought to myself, *you're the one filing for divorce.*

"It's your job to tell me these things! I was having second thoughts for a minute or two and then I saw this shit. If she's been cheating on me I'm going to make this divorce a living hell for her. And if you know something and you're not telling me, then you're going to be in trouble as well, I promise you that."

I could feel my heart pounding, I had never been threatened or spoken to like that by *A* before and with *B* recently having called me a worthless amoeba, my share price as a celebrity assistant was falling rapidly.

"I promise you this is nothing to be worked up about, it's just gossip. You know how these so called journalists work. Focus on your movie and I'll see to it that she calls you as soon as she can." I don't know why I said this, because I was putting myself in all kinds of possible trouble, but I'd been caught off guard and way outside my comfortable lying zone.

When I got back to the table I found Cesar and Luís talking animatedly and sounding almost like old buddies. "Sorry, business call," I said and held up my phone.

"This guy is amazing!" Cesar said with a grin as wide as his face, "Just wait until you hear this." He put the iPad and headphones in front me. I sat down and opened my mouth, but I didn't know what to say. It wasn't in the plan to encourage the kid, we were supposed to shoot him down gently. I gave Cesar an angry stare, which he of course didn't register, then I sighed and put on the headphones. The situation had spun out of control and there was nothing to do but listen to Luís song and then hopefully figure something out.

The video player started and at first the screen was pitch black. Then a spotlight was turned on and a muted bass beat started thumping in the background. A few seconds later another spotlight came on and a muted piano began clinking a looping melody. It was all surprisingly nicely produced, but I guess Jorge's talk had lowered my expectations a great deal.

After the fifth and last spotlight had been switched on, a man walked out of the darkness and into the light, wearing a red hoodie, a pair of beat-up jeans and a big, red, oversized baseball cap. This was Luís of course. He opened his mouth and let out a soft wailing sound and although I

was prepared *not* to like it (I kind of wanted not to like it) -
I did. Only 30 seconds into the song even a layman such as
myself could see that the guy had talent.

"...*and aiiiaiiiiaiiiiijjjjj*...am born a star." was how, about
four minutes later, the song ended. I was speechless. Luís
had just blown me away and I had no idea how to react. I
had promised his father to dismiss him gently, but how
could I do that after what I'd just seen?

I nodded my head in silence, returned Luís' iPad to him,
and looked over at Cesar who seemed eager to hear
something.

"Well?" he said and looked at me.

"Fantastic," I stumbled out.

Then Cesar turned to Luís: "Young man," he said, "I
think I can speak for both of us when I say I'm very
impressed by this performance. You sure have a special
talent and I think we can help you exploit it." Cesar's voice
was unwavering, determined and believable. For anyone
except for yours truly, who depended on what he was going
to say.

"We can obviously not *promise* anything here," I said in
a hurry, "the competition is extremely tough and there's a
lot of young talent like yourself out there. But I agree with
my partner that this was a powerful performance."

Cesar didn't seem to hear me, "Is this on Youtube? Or do
you have a plan to upload it?"

I could see that the kid, who had just finished his
sandwich, was actually quite ecstatic and surprised by our
praise for his song. He had this smirk on his face which
seemed impossible to suppress: "I have thought of doing it,
but when my father told me about this opportunity I
wanted to show it to you first. You're kind of the first people

to see it. Do you think I should put it out there?"

Cesar was fast and answered like he'd gotten this question many times before, "I would advice you to wait with that, I'm going to check some contacts first, think about our possibilities and we'll get back to you."

I had no idea what Cesar was talking about and neither did he. Still he kept on talking.

"Would it be possible for you to e-mail or dropbox us this clip?"

"Sure! I'll do it straight away," Luís said, enthusiastically. Cesar then gave him the fake e-mail address he had created for this purpose, which would redirect straight into his own Gmail account. I witnessed this in confusion, but was powerless to stop it.

"As I understood it, you're planning on participating in American Idol?" Cesar the fake music company CEO said, looking as serious as ever.

"Yeah, I thought it could get the name out, open up possibilities, stuff like that."

Cesar lowered his voice, "Again, I think you should take it easy, let's see what we can work on first. I'm sure we can set up something for you."

"Sounds good," Luis said, but I'm sure he would have agreed to pretty much anything at this stage, that's how excited he was.

"Great. We'll get back to you as soon as we can," Cesar said and casually asked the waiter for the bill. I looked over at Luís, who had dollar signs in his eyes. I bet he couldn't wait to tell his friends about this amazingly positive meeting with the powerful music execs.

We all shook hands and said bye to the artist formerly known as Jorge's son and when the kid was out of hearsay,

I gave Cesar a stern look and said: "Now what the fuck was that about? Do you want to pump the guy up to make his fall harder or what? Did you completely forget what the plan was?"

"*Au contraire*, my dear Watson, I just had a severe epiphany when I listened to his stuff - this guy is really talented! He has definitely got the potential and *you*'re going to help him become a star."

"What?"

Cesar's eyes were the size of Ping-Pong balls, which made me wonder if he had snorted something prior to the meeting, "Don't you see it? This can be your big break! Your chance to wrestle your sorry self free from your assistant lifestyle and do something different, something fun and possibly *huge!*"

Somewhere in the back of my mind I appreciated my friend trying to know what was best for me and my so called career, but at this stage it was becoming too much to handle. "How could I be an agent for this kid? It would be detrimental to both of us. Besides, I'm feeling really bad going against his father's wish."

Cesar finished his pint and started rubbing his scalp again. I didn't care if it was just a nervous twitch or a hint of nostalgia, it was pretty annoying. But it turned out Cesar was even more annoyed with me and my outlook on things, "Just listen to you! You're such a wimp! Take some risks for once, will you? You told me about this guy Barry, big shot in music - how lucky you are to have a contact like that! And what a fucking coincidence! Give him a call, set up a meeting, show him what you've got. Being an agent to a young music prodigy sounds a helluva lot sexier and lucrative than being an assistant to some crazy actress."

At first I wanted to retaliate, but after letting it sink in for a couple of seconds, I realized that in a way he was right, maybe this *was* a great opportunity for me. In my rather sketchy situation with *B*, a divorce, a mysterious lover and lord knows what else, it actually made sense to give it a shot.

I looked at Cesar who was watching my reaction desperately and I said: "Maybe you're right."

And after that we ordered another round of beers and with each sip the plan was starting to sound better. A major change in my life edged closer and I was getting more and more excited about it. Little did I know what kind of change it would become.

***

Jorge didn't sound very convinced about what I just had told him. No, his anger levels were not far from the time when the main oven broke down in the middle of preparing for a big show-off dinner at the Johnson mansion, "You told him he actually has talent? Why did you do that, Darryl?"

"Because I honestly believe so. I've even booked a meeting with Barry Waldruff to show him his video. That's how good I think it is." This wasn't hundred percent true, at the time I was still waiting on a confirmation from Barry's secretary.

"But how do you know he's good? You don't have any experience in the music industry. I'm really disappointed you didn't come to me first."

"I find your lack of faith disturbing," I said in a nervous and awful imitation of Darth Vader, "I know this might sound crazy to you, but I think it's definitely worth a shot and if it doesn't work out, then Luís at least got the opportunity. And if that happens, I will let him down as gently as I can and to be honest with you, I see no harm in him doing American Idol. He's good enough to win it and not bad enough to make a fool out of himself."

Jorge was quiet for a while, probably wondering what to think about his friend running wild with his son's farfetched dreams, then he said, "You're a good friend and I of course trust your judgment, but this is my son we're talking about and I don't want him to get hurt or waste his time on something that will never work. Do you really think he's that good?"

"I do, Jorge, I really do."

"Well, let's just pray you're right. And if you make my son's dream come true when I doubted him, I will be forever grateful to you. But please keep me in the loop."

"Of course."

We ended the phone call and I was happy I'd managed to convince him, although I still needed to convince myself. Things were moving too fast and I felt that, though they could end up absolutely fine, I didn't have control and could equally well find myself in the other end of the line rather soon.

***

Before I met with Barry, I wanted to tell *B* about my plans. After all, she was the only reason I got an appointment with him in the first place. He simply hadn't gotten over his crush for her yet. For him she was the woman who had eluded him, something which few women had done before thanks to nothing but his money and power. Because no matter how fat, disgusting and remarkably unattractive he was, there were always a few young girls in skimpy clothing close to him. But *B* had always thought he was a pig, so no matter how hard he tried, he would never snatch as much as a kiss from her.

I didn't care if Barry was a pig or not, he was the only natural way I could get my new career rolling. I needed to work fast, because I didn't know how things stood with *B*, we hadn't talked properly since she yelled at me for stalking her and I had no clue how she felt about things. I knew I needed to tell her what was going on and she had via text message agreed to have a drink with me at the famous King Cole bar terrace.

I wanted to dress extra nicely for the occasion and had bought a new beige blazer and a black shirt, admittedly from Gap and with my own money (I didn't feel like extending my expense card privilege anymore), but it was still an effort. I arrived early, sat down at the table I had reserved and ordered a glass of Pinot Noir. I was very nervous.

I had never gone to King Cole before, which I felt sad about as soon as I sat down and looked around. The ambiance was spectacular: classy, elegant, warm, and with lots of personality soaked up through the history of the place. I could easily have spent half-an-hour just studying the beautifully painted and massive mural hanging over the elongated and carved oak bar.

B had of course been here before, or at least that was what it seemed like with her rushing in, looking flustered and annoyed and almost falling into her chair. As usual she gathered the attention from the other patrons, but probably not for the "right" reasons.

It felt strange seeing her. Not that it was long ago, but a whole lot had happened since we came to New York and I'd gone from being over-my-head in love with her, to contemplating leaving her side. *B*, on one hand, was married when she arrived in New York, and had had to suddenly readjust to thinking she was single again. Not that she was only a *victim* of that equation, she hadn't exactly been a relationship role-model herself. And when it came to our relationship, our friendship, nothing seemed certain anymore. I had stalked her, she had shouted mean things at me, she was moving and had originally wanted me to move with her. What she wanted to do at any point in time, only she could know.

"Hi Darryl," she said in a forced voice as she sat down. For a second I felt sorry for her, for no particular reason.

"You look dazzling," I said, trying to sound both upbeat and relaxed, carefully masking my dangling strings of nerves.

"Thanks. Glad you like it. I had my doubts about this green, but I think it works," she said, suddenly not looking so upset.

A waiter passed by and *B* asked for a glass of pink Moet. Obviously.

I suddenly felt frozen, with no idea of what I was going to say. I had a clear battle plan when I came, but when it was crunch time I started doubting myself. Thankfully, B began the proceedings.

"Before you say anything...I saw the papers. *A* has called me twenty times and you were stalking me the other night. I know what's going on. You all seem to be thinking I'm sleeping around."

No beating around the bush here. With *B* you never

needed an ice-breaker, more like a helmet.

"Is it strange? You looked very much in love in those pictures. And I think it was a very unnecessary thing to do, you knew there was a huge risk those pictures were going to be circling the Internet today. You're in the early stages of a divorce and ought to tread more carefully." I tried to sound like I only meant her best and that I came in peace, but it was hard to mask the hurt in my voice. I just couldn't shut my feelings off either, they were still there, I was just trying to run away from them.

"Right now, I honestly couldn't give a shit what people think. I'm not saying it's true, but so what if I'm seeing Matteo? I'm sure *A* is not being the best boy around the movie set. I hear stuff too, you know."

"He told me he was considering getting back together before he saw the pictures."

"He said that? What glorious bullshit. A bird whispered in my ear he's already shagging a younger actress. So if he wants to make a hassle about our divorce, let me tell you that two can play that game!" *B* sipped her champagne with determination, she appeared stressed and unhappy and I couldn't help but think back to Rome and simpler, more beautiful times.

Days ago.

"So what are you going to do?" Now that I'd completely lost my footing, all I had were more questions.

"Nothing changes. We're going to get a divorce and I'm going to move here." *B*'s tone was short and frosty. It was not one of our nicest times together. I decided to go straight for the elephant in the room.

"First you screamed at me and then you woke up in my bed? What was that about?"

"I realize that was weird and I'm sorry. I was lonely and drunk and felt bad for shouting at you. I guess you only had my best in mind."

"I always have your best in mind."

"Did you have my best in mind when you called up Barry Waldruff to book a meeting without telling me?"

B's voice hit me like the recoil from a gun. If she had known this all along she really was a talented actress. I guess I had some explaining to do.

I took a deep breath and prepared to meet her cold stare, "Well, I met with Jorge's son Luís the other day and it turns out he's a major RnB talent. I'm not kidding - he's really good! So as a favor to Jorge I've booked a meeting with Barry to see if I can get him signed." The cat was out of the bag, but *B*'s frosty glare was still there.

"Like his agent?"

"I don't know. Maybe. Something like that. It's a long-shot, but I'm doing it as a favor to Jorge. We'll see what happens." My idea was starting to sound more and more farfetched for every second *B* gave me that look. What had Cesar pushed me into? Not that this was all his fault, I had gotten carried away too.

"Sorry Darryl, but this plan of yours sounds absolutely ridiculous to me. You have zero experience in music and suddenly think you might help a kid score a record deal?"

The wine had developed a sour taste along with the conversation, "I just said it would be stupid to miss out on this opportunity."

"What happens if you manage to get him signed, then?" As she waved the waiter over for more champagne, I felt disappointment wash over me. Disappointment at myself for getting so excited about such a crazy idea, but also sadness for her going out of her way to belittle my chances of doing something new and different. Maybe this wasn't really friendship after all, maybe it was just a job, I thought. Maybe I was stupid?

B took a brisk sip from her champagne, she was anxious and edgy now, ready to snap. I wished I could have turned the clock 20 minutes backwards. Or 20 days backwards.

"I don't know what happens. I guess I'll help him out with his career a bit, I think I can do both." I knew this sounded ridiculous, but I wasn't in control of the situation, which meant I wasn't in control of my mouth either.

"I honestly thought you were smarter than this," she said in a sharp voice, "You can't be my assistant and the agent for some kid, that doesn't work and we both know it. I think this sounds like you want to leave me. You wouldn't have thought of this crazy idea if you weren't."

B was now feeling lonely and insecure, which often turned her into a nasty person. She was right in her reasoning though, if I was perfectly happy where I was, I probably wouldn't have done this in the first place. But then I didn't know if I was unhappy because of her unreturned feelings or if I was just tired of my job. Or both.

"B, I have no idea what's going to happen. Like I said, there's a high possibility that nothing comes out of it. I just wanted to tell you what's going on, nothing more. It's not a big deal."

She suddenly had this vacant look in her eyes, like all the positive energy she had collected in Rome had been drained from her. "I can't deal with this right now, I can't even look at you."

Then she took her chunky Gucci bag and rushed out of King Cole, leaving me alone with her empty glass and a mouthful of guilt.

***

It was going down, well, I was actually going *up* in the elevator of Barry's headquarters, anxious like a coke-head who'd just found a 100-dollar bill. I had brought my laptop, a USB-stick with Luís' video, my best suit, my Hugo Boss leather shoulder bag, everything to look the part. You could say I was ready to rumble, in fact my stomach already did.

When I reached the correct floor and the stainless steel elevator doors opened, I found myself in front of a huge, marble slab of a reception desk where Barry Waldruff's secretary and assistant, Jacqueline, held court. Jacqueline had a fierce personality (over the phone) and short, boyish, brown hair, thick lips and beautiful mocha skin, sort of like Halle Berry, except further away from a smile. Working for Barry probably did that to you. She looked at me in a way that spelled out, *"Now who the hell is this lowlife?"*

A fair question. And that was why I had donned my new suit and really put care into my appearance, because I knew that with Barry you really needed to make an impression. I had never had a longer conversation than a couple of sentences with him, but I had picked up on his body language and heard some of his famous anecdotes from afar. It was enough to know that he was the kind of person even his own mother thinks is an asshole.

But he was a rich and powerful asshole and that's why I was paying him a visit.

"Mr. Waldruff will be available in a few minutes, Mr. Glendale. Please have a seat." Jacqueline said, more of an order than a suggestion. I sat down in one of the black leather chairs and felt my heart jolt. I hadn't been this nervous since the first day with B. It was good they had the air condition on the freezer setting, because I was sweating profusely.

After a few minutes wait, the massive oak doors in front of me opened and out waddled Barry, his blazer big enough for me to camp in and his cheeks red and flabby like hanging slabs of meat. He looked like a man ready to explode.

"Darryl, right?" He reached out a thick arm and shook my hand so hard I was afraid he was going to yank it out of its socket.

I said yes, posed a weak smile and followed him into his office, which offered a fantastic view of the Empire State building and was big enough to have an almost full-size putting green in it (an 80s executive cliché if there ever was one). The walls were lined with gold and platinum albums and plenty of pictures of himself, shaking hands with famous people.

"Pretty wow, huh?" he said, congratulating himself.

"Yeah, it's spectacular," I said, while I did my best not to throw up. It was not only nerves, Barry also made me physically sick to my stomach.

He walked over to a mahogany cabinet in the corner and brought out a crystal flask of amber-colored liquid. He took out two matching glasses, poured them to the middle mark and handed me one without asking if I wanted it or not. "So Darryl, this is quite a surprise for me, I didn't think you had anything to do with the music industry."

The derogatory tone wasn't helping my confidence, but I took a breath and told myself that *here goes absolutely nothing*. Zero, in fact.

"Well, to be honest with you Barry, I never *had* much to do with it. The movie industry I've learned quite a bit about through my work with *B*, but the music industry, no. But I think there are similarities between the two and I thought this opportunity was too good to miss out on."

Barry sucked in a huge gulp of brandy and let out a long and disgusting *aaaaaaaah*, "You know, I never really do this kind of meetings anymore. I'm too busy and I've learned that most people who think they know talent when they hear it, don't understand jack shit about this business." Barry sat down in his chair and studied me like I was a zit on his leg.

"Yes, I understand that and I'm really thankful you took the time."

"I honestly didn't remember you one bit at first, but after thinking for a while I got a vague image in my head. *B*'s assistant, *B*'s assistant, I was racking my brains. Then I remembered you were her beloved black friend and that she had actually spoken very highly of you. And since she is very dear to my heart, I couldn't really say no could I? So I was shocked by the phone call I got from her not long ago."

Black friend? Thank you Barry, it's always nice to be color coded. But seriously, what phone call? I thought, still sweating.

"She said I should avoid doing business with you, that you don't know what you're talking about." Barry walked around his office with his hands in his pocket, like a predator circling his prey. "I don't really know what to make of all this, Darryl, do you?"

I was left speechless, shocked to the core that *B* would do such a thing to me, if only to stop the possibility that I might leave her or whatever her evil plan was.

I stuttered, "To be honest with you Barry, I just think she's really worried I might resign as a result of it and that's probably why she called you. I see no other reason for her trying to trip me up like this, because I promise you I really brought something interesting with me and it's well worth listening to." I was trying to sound calm, but I was both furious and embarrassed.

"That's for me to decide," said Barry. He might not have listened completely to her, but he was obviously affected by it, which I hoped didn't damage Luís chances too much. After all, I was pretty sure Barry put business before all kinds of personal drama and if he saw a chance to make money - you could be pretty sure he was going to take it.

"Of course," I said with as much humility as I could muster.

"Give me the fucking thing then, let's see what this kid is worth."

I handed him the USB-stick and he put it in his laptop and clicked a few times on the mousepad, and seconds later, on the massive screen behind me, Luís video to his song "Bornastar" started.

I was too nervous to look at Barry's reactions, so I watched the video for something like the tenth time. Despite the predictable and silly lyrics, I still thought it was a pretty damn good melody and performance and I hoped Barry felt the same way. My prediction was that Luís, with his stage charisma and strong voice, had real star quality.

When the video stopped, the music mogul seemed lost in thought for a few seconds. His massive cheeks were fluttering like curtains in the breeze. I expected two things; either for him to lash out at me for bringing him crap or telling me it was time to make money. He pulled out the

USB-stick from his laptop, handed it to me and said, "The kid's got talent, no doubt about that," he paused, keeping my hopes up, "his voice is good, but sadly not original enough to make it in this do-or-die music world. There are too many similar artists around and the style is kind of 2008. We're looking for something fresh. But I guess you'd known this if you were more connected to the business."

My heart sank. *What was I thinking?* That I could sell something to a guy like Barry just because Cesar and I, two guys with no music business experience whatsoever, liked it? It was definitely on my top five list of naive things to do and all I could do was to face the music (or the lack of it) and deal with this disappointing situation.

But first, I needed to beg a little, "You really think there's nothing in this? You can't give him some feedback, let him work on it, make him into something. The guy is really talented, has a strong personality and good looks." I tried, desperately.

Barry thought I was wasting his time, "He just doesn't have it. My answer is no."

I thanked Barry for the meeting and told him to call me if he changed his mind.

The fat man chuckled, "I never change my mind, about anything. I'm pure gut through and through (*you could say that again!*) and that's what made me successful. But I wish you all the best nonetheless and send my love to *B* when you see her. If you see her." Barry laughed like he'd just told a joke. Apparently my misfortunes were funny.

I exited Barry's office dejected. I knew I should probably have been happy that I went through with it, that I gave it a shot, but the air had completely gone out of me. I simply couldn't believe how *B* had tried to derail me, it was really a

167

bomb on what I'd always thought was a great working relationship and a strong friendship. A person I thought I loved, who I had done so much for, just cut me down like I was no more than a damaged strand of hair. How could I work for a person like that? I was fine with her having all the tantrums in the world, but this was something else.

Anger and frustration aside, I took the bull by the horns and called Luís about the news right away and wished him the best of luck in the upcoming Idol auditions. At least he had that to look forward to and I knew he could do well there, after all, even Barry said he had talent. "I'll watch you on TV soon then," I said and we ended the call on a positive note, despite Luís obvious disappointment.

But even though one uncomfortable call was done, I still felt like shit. What was I going to do? I couldn't really work for B anymore could I? Not after all this.

And as I was walking down Madison Ave, I thought I'd rather flip burgers than pick up another celebrity turd with my bare hands.

The problem was, I needed more time. Just a little more time.

***

I hadn't talked to *B* in 24 hours, but in an effort to try and patch things up between us, I had agreed to join her for a walk in Central Park after I'd picked up the keys to her new apartment. I'd tossed and turned through a very long night, wrestling with the thought of breaking free or whatever I was about to do. It was the most difficult decision of my life. But in the end I had reached the conclusion to stay for a few months more and plan my exit a bit better. I wasn't a fan of rash decisions.

The atmosphere was tense and icy from the first step together and I could sense how annoyed she was at me. At me! For doing what? For trying to stand up for myself? At this point, I could only see the dark side of *B*, the way she always put herself first in every equation. She saw my talk about possibly carving out a new career for myself as betrayal, nothing else.

We walked briskly in our colorful Nike trainers and were starting to build up a sweat, when, right around the Turtle Pond, I threw the first punch.

"That thing you did when you called Barry and shot me down, it wasn't nice." Understatement of the year nominee. But although I had decided to stay with her, I wanted to make my point across. I was too angry not to.

"You mean how you tried to backstab me and use one of my contacts to weasel yourself into a new career was nice then?" Her reply was fast and I could tell she felt as worked up about this as I was.

"I didn't backstab you! I told you about my plans, an idea that, possibly thanks to you, in the end didn't pan out. I had to do something! You're falling apart and you don't seem one bit interested in stopping it. I've tried so hard to help you, but in the end you can only help yourself." I hesitated to mention how let-down I felt when I thought we were getting closer and she stabbed me in the heart by hooking up with the Italian Stallion.

"Darryl, as usual you're right. I can only help myself. I have to stop relying on this fucked-up celebrity safety system I've built up around myself. I'm an adult person. I don't need a team. I can do things myself and I can deal with my own problems."

"What's that supposed to mean?"

"I think it's time I try to be completely independent. At least as far as possible. I have expected too much from you throughout the years and like it is, it's impossible to stay friends and work together. I need some time to figure things out myself and that's why I'm relieving you of your duties. You're obviously on your way somewhere else anyway."

I had made up my to stay with her, but with the intention of also making her aware of how much she had hurt me. I had expected remorse, tears, an apology - but instead she was firing me! *What the fuck!* I was shocked by her heartlessness. Whatever crush I'd had on her was being beaten to death by her cold behavior and whatever chemistry we'd felt was being wiped out completely. Left were only two very frustrated people with two very unclear futures. Mine slightly more shady, to say the least.

"So you want me to leave now? Today? Pack my stuff and go?" I said this with my voice cracking, she had pulled my legs from under me and I was abruptly falling into the abyss of the unknown.

B's voice was suddenly reminiscent of her mother's, "Take your time, but the sooner the better. I'm moving into the apartment and you can stay in the suite for a while, that's fine. And don't think I'm not thankful for what you've done for me, I just need to deal with this alone. I hope you understand."

And where I had expected tears, *B* just increased the speed in her step and left me standing there, without even as much as goodbye.

***

Four months later

Stepping onto North Herndon Road near Clarendon Metro in Arlington, Virginia, was like walking down memory lane. I don't care how tired and old the metaphor is, it's the only one which really captures the feeling properly. I had lived there throughout my childhood and kissed my first girl not far from there, Megan, a freckled strawberry blonde with braces. In first grade I learned how to ride a bike there, the marine-blue Scott mountain-bike with 18 gears that I loved and rode to death. Waves of memories came tumbling in and out of my head, giving me heavy bouts of nostalgia and dragging me almost physically down to my roots.

Almost four months had passed since I got my things from LA and sealed the chapter of my employment with the Johnsons. Everything went relatively smooth, at least for a break-up. I collected my stuff in LA, thanked *A* and the gang for my time there (Jorge and I shared a choked-up word over a beer), took my Prius and drove towards Virginia and my parents' house in Clarendon. Success wasn't riding in the car with me, quite the opposite. I had lost the job I'd fought so hard for and instead of throwing myself into the search for a new one, I'd made up my mind to go home. I needed distance more than anything else.

It would be nice to say that I never looked back, but it was exactly what I did. I felt ashamed for how things had unravelled with *B*. We had always had something strong together, a rare working friendship and it hurt me to have lost it so suddenly. We hadn't talked in months, but not a day passed by without me thinking of her and the many great times we had together. It's true what they say, you never know what you have until it's gone.

Where did we go wrong? I don't know. Falling in love with her and stalking her wasn't of much help. But, of course, she was the one who went crazy first, drinking like a sponge, not paying attention to her marriage and ultimately falling apart on the red carpet. She had travelled on a hell of a downward spiral and I had gotten caught in the whirlwind. In a way I could excuse myself by saying I'd only been one of the casualties in the drama she had created for herself.

But it was hard to see it like that when I missed her like crazy.

All I knew about her current situation was what I'd heard from Fredric. He had called me asking if I had any good job contacts since *A* had wanted a fresh start and was trying to sell the house in an effort to cut all the strings to his ex-wife. I had told Fredric to maybe go to New York and ask B for a job, but he'd said she was a little too much to handle on his own.

I had also tried to call *B* twice just to talk for a bit and see what's up, but she hadn't picked up the phone. I didn't know what she was trying to do except to shut me out, but my feeling about it wasn't good. I was very worried about her.

But maybe I should have focused more on myself, as it was a bit strange to be almost 30 years old and live with your parents, especially not after a life as a high-profile celebrity assistant. Although I took some comfort in that I knew it wasn't bad enough to last very long. A few months was what I needed to clear my head and make up my mind on what to do next.

The dream of my wine bar was of course still there,

albeit a bit different. I'd thought that LA could work for it, but returning to Virginia made me realize I wasn't missing California one bit. If I was going to go into the restaurant business, it had to be in a place where I could make a big buzz and the only place that made sense was New York. Sadly, I needed more money to even think about the Big Apple. That was also one of the reasons I started working for my father, helping him with his building business, making some money and saving almost every cent. It convinced me I was still on track.

I could of course have stayed in New York, moved in with Cesar and taken some job. But I needed my space and my time away from B. And then it became too late, because Cesar's girlfriend moved in with him. His happiness was evident the few times we talked over Skype or phone, and although I was happy for my friend, I couldn't help but feel jealous too. How could things have turned out so smoothly for him and not for me?

But then, one day, when I was sitting in my parents' beige and worn leather sofa, enjoying a glass of wine (cheaper than what I was used to, but good anyway) after a day of hard manual labour with my father's firm, my mother was calling my name. I turned down the sound of the old LP player (which was spinning "The Best of James Brown") and shouted back at her: "What is it?"

"Someone's here to see you." My mouther shouted back.

I walked over to the hallway, and outside, on the doorstep, stood B with a brown shoulder bag slung over her shoulder and a grey trench coat hanging on her skinny frame. She had lost weight and looked haggard and tired.

"Hi," she said when she saw me. Just hi.

"I'll let you two talk," my mother sensed the privacy

needed and walked back to the kitchen.

"Hi," I said, my voice unsteady.

"I've come all this way, can I at least come in?"

"Yeah, sure." I said, in shock and stood aside to let the movie star enter my parents' modest house.

***

B stayed in my parents' guest room that night. We all had dinner together, my mother fretting out about not being able to cook something better than a spaghetti bolognese for the superstar, but *B* said she loved it and that she was very happy to sit down in a *real* family setting for once in a while. She seemed comfortable around us, which made me happy. My father was visibly affected by her "star glow" and I could sense how impressed he was that I'd struck such a chord with someone as successful as her, at least strong enough for her to travel all the way to Clarendon alone to see me. He offered her a glass from his finest whisky (he's quite a collector) but she declined politely and said she was staying away from alcohol for time being. I looked at her face, which had a couple of new lines from last time I saw her and thought, *good for you*.

After dinner, which mostly involved my parents asking shallow questions about her and her movies, I suggested *B* and I go for a walk. She gladly agreed, probably looking forward to speak in private.

We passed my old playground (the same old rusty swing still there), while B told me the story on how she fell on dark days as soon as both *A* and I left her to her own devices. She cried, drank and painted a lot. She said I was right all along about Matteo and his intentions and that he "imposed" himself on her and that she, in her need for company and any kind of love, fell for it.

Matteo turned out to be more into her fame and lifestyle than her person so she kicked him out of the apartment after a few weeks and then got even more depressed about the lack of love and human interaction in her life. She thought of calling *A* and begging him to take her back, but by then the magazines had already told the story about his new girlfriend and she didn't stomach it. Instead she drank even more and spent the days "trying to capture herself on canvas", like any true and depressed artist. This often ended up with her stamping the foot through what she was working on or just laying on the couch in her apartment, trying to cure monster hangovers.

B looked at me with tears in her eyes as we walked past three young boys shooting hoops in the schoolyard, "I was slowly killing myself," she said. "At first I was so excited to be in New York, to experience the city full out and be the truly independent girl I always wanted to be, but it's not easy to do that when you're...well, me."

"So what made you come here?"

"I don't know. I guess one day I just felt it was either death or getting out, getting away from my own demons, the strange pressure I've been putting on myself my entire life. I thought I could fix it on my own, but that turned out to be far from true. Actually the only one who can relieve this pressure without expecting anything in return, is you. I know I treated you like shit and I feel awful for doing that. You're the only person who has never judged me and I need that. For me, that has become the most important feeling in the world."

I didn't know how to react. It warmed my heart to hear

how she valued me and my support, but then she didn't know that I *had* wanted something back from her, I had wanted love. But we had gotten passed that so I said nothing and just held out my arms and hugged her for a long time while I let her tears dry against my shirt.

***

That night I had a vivid nightmare. I dreamt I entered *B*'s New York apartment and found her dead, in the bathtub, her wrists cut and her body lying in a pool of blood. I jumped up from my sleep and felt my heart beat heavy inside my chest. I tried to fall asleep again, but couldn't. I was afraid of falling back into that horrible dream. I turned on the light and after a few minutes of just lying there, looking up at the ceiling and trying not to think, I heard a faint sound. *Tock-tock.* My heart jumped again. Was it raining or were there just some old floorboards creaking? I heard the sound again and rose from my puny bed and walked over to my bedroom window to look for drops of rain. Then I heard a whisper, "Darryl...Darryl."

I opened the door to find B standing there in a short, red silk robe. "You're awake?" she said.

"Yeah, well, obviously," I replied.

"I couldn't sleep either, can I come in?" And without waiting for my reply, she entered my bedroom.

She sat down on my bed, "Your bed is so cute. I can really see you sleeping here as a kid."

"If you mean cute like in small, yes, I guess it's cute. I don't know if it's cute that I sleep here now though." I said and smiled nervously. Making jokes out of my own misfortune was my trusted defense mechanism.

"It's not that small. Would you mind if we just lay down a bit and talk or try to sleep? You know I'm no good with sleeping alone."

I didn't know what to say to that. I *did* know that *B* wasn't very good with being alone, that's why it made sense that her whole adventure of going it alone in New York didn't work out.

"Well, yeah, sure - unless you want to grab a tea or warm milk or something? My parents are in the other end of the corridor and they won't hear us if we go downstairs for a bit." I said and felt 15 years old.

"I'd rather just lay down for a bit if that's okay."

"Okay."

We laid down next to each other in my small bed, which was impossible to fit two people in without them touching. I felt her naked leg against mine and suddenly my blood started rushing. Rushing downhill.

"Darryl, do you mind holding me for a bit? I'm freezing."

I like to sleep in cold rooms and often have the air condition turned down low, but my room had no air condition and it wasn't particularly cold. I thought of offering her the whole bed, not to poke her and embarrass myself again, but before I could say anything, she positioned herself close and brushed the pointiest part of my body.

"But Darryl," she said in a light and humorous voice, "Are you *that* happy to see me?" Then she giggled and I felt her hand reach down.

Oh, I thought.

***

The next day I woke with an aching back and *B* next to me, wheezing toxic air from her mouth, but her face more peaceful and beautiful than ever. I was wedged between her and the wall, but using all the strength in my arms, I managed to get out of bed without waking her.

I walked across the hall to the bathroom and took a long shower, relieving some of the strain in my back with the hot water. I was still really tired, but in a good, post-intercourse, way. I didn't know what to think of the night before, I was just happy it happened. Whether or not it would happen again, was up for *B* to decide.

I knew I would gladly oblige.

After the shower I went back to my room and got dressed, while *B* slept soundly and then I headed downstairs for a cup of coffee. It was Saturday, so I wasn't surprised to find my parents around the kitchen table, reading different parts of the newspaper with their reading glasses on. It was a friendly and familiar image.

"Morning," they said when they saw me approach the table, "She's still asleep?" My mother smiled like it was my child we were talking about.

"Think so," I said, not wanting to divulge the information that *B* slept next to me (and on top of me) and not in the guest room.

"She's such a nice girl, why can't you find yourself someone like her," my mother suddenly burst out, almost like she knew.

"Yeah, she is," I said, "complicated, but nice."

"Show me a woman who isn't," my father shot back, chuckled and touched my mother on her shoulder like she would be the first one to agree. It was a gesture of love I was thankful to see; a reminder that true love could actually last. My folks had been going strong for more than thirty years, something that was becoming increasingly rare.

"True," I said and poured myself a cup of coffee, "Any good news today?" I looked towards the newspaper spread around the kitchen table.

"If you want good news I don't think you should read the paper, son." My father said, without looking up.

I popped two slices of white bread in the toaster and looked out of the kitchen window and on my parents' lawn. I used to play all kinds of sports out there when I was kid, it had truly been my playground then, but gone back to being just a lawn. A lawn in need of a trim.

I sipped the strong and acidic coffee, which was how my father had taken it for 35 years. He was built like a bull and not exactly what you would call a *latte person*. But the bull looked softer than a puppy when *B* entered the kitchen in her red silk robe and Four Seasons slippers. She sure knew how to melt the heart of men (and the brains of husbands and employees).

"Good morning," she said, stretched and yawned like a cat. It was like it was the most natural thing for her to be walking around in my parent's house wearing practically nothing. And it looked like my father could get used to it.

"Good morning," my mother said, either not witnessing my father's stare, or just choosing to ignore it. I knew they really liked her, so I wasn't worried about her presence here, in fact it felt oddly comfortable, like it was how it was meant to be. If you scrap the living-with-the-parents thing.

B sat down by the kitchen table and I put a freshly-poured cup of ulcer coffee in front of her without saying anything. My tongue was suddenly stuck to my throat. In many ways we knew each other like a married couple, but things usually changed as soon as you started sleeping together.

"Thanks," she said and gave me a flirtatious little smile. Something stirred inside of me.

"Slept well?" My father asked, trying to sound his casual self, despite having a celebrity at the breakfast table.

"Yes, like a baby," *B* said, sounding chipper, "I can't begin to tell you how much this means to me, how good it feels to be around a loving family for a change."

I remember telling my parents about *B*'s own family situation, so they knew what she was talking about. "We're really happy to have you here as well and you should feel like you're always welcome in our home. I just wish I'd been able to clean up first," my mother said looking around the room, seeing dust and mess where nobody else could. This is a mother's superhuman ability, among others.

"But you have a lovely home, I absolutely adore this house, it's so cute." Everything small but not too small, was "cute" to *B*. I had a hard time seeing my parents' house objectively though, it was too ingrained in my system - the smells, the carpets, I think even the old sofa had become a part of me.

"I'm glad you like it," my father said, "we've lived here for 30 years now and hopefully we can live here the rest of our lives." He looked over at my mother who nodded her head. They were proud to call it home.

"I envy you, Darryl, you must have had that childhood everybody wants." *B*'s voice tailed off a bit on the end and I could feel the honesty in her pain - this was the kind of family life she'd been missing all along. The one who shared breakfast around the kitchen table.

"I know," I said and sat down, "I'm one lucky guy," and I looked at my parents who smiled back. And I did feel that way, I *was* lucky.

"Would you mind," *B* said, in her modest I'm-asking-you-a-favor voice, "if I stayed here a few more days? Would that be okay with you guys?"

I was relieved to hear this, because in my head I had feared she would be taking the first flight back.

"Of course - stay as long as you like," my mother said, probably hearing wedding bells somewhere in the back of her head. They hadn't seen me with a girl in a long time, a void my mother was desperate to fill - it had been far too obvious in the way she talked to me.

"Great, I really love it here. It's so nice and down-to-earth and normal in the best possible way."

And I was of course happy to have her there too, although to me, when I saw her sitting at our old kitchen table in that short, red silk robe, looking like a million bucks - "normal" was out the door. ***

My head was a mess over the coming days as I was trying to block myself from falling head over heels back in love with a re-energized and relaxed *B*. I tried desperately not to get too high, because I knew how much harder the fall back to reality would be. I simply didn't want to get hurt, but it wasn't easy not to be endeared by the happy, humorous girl who acted in all those romantic comedies for a reason - when she was in this mood, it was almost impossible *not* to fall for her.

So what do you do when a Hollywood superstar decides to move in with you and your parents? How do you relax and pretend like everything's normal? That it's not some lucky spell, bound to end with the flick of the same wand which brought her there? You can't. One minute you're floating on clouds and the next you're walking on eggshells, afraid the illusion you're so blissfully in will go *poff!* - up in smoke. I obviously didn't know what to do, so I focused on helping her relax and making sure she wouldn't go back into the destructive mood that created the situation in the first place. We took long walks, watched movies, talked a lot and every night she came into my room to sleep with me and later also by my side. We didn't kiss or anything like that during the daytime, but she didn't hesitate to take my hand or ask me to hold her when we were alone. Although I loved this state of being, I realized we couldn't stay this way forever, so I needed to pop the question, where were we going with this?

"Where are we going with what?" B of course knew what I meant, she was just buying herself more time for an answer.

"With us? What's next? Or do you want to move into my boyhood room permanently?" I said, trying to make the conversation as light as it could be, but of course my nerves were dangling like telephone wires in a storm.

"I don't know. It's too early, too confusing. Right now I only know I want you near me. I'm sorry, but that's all I can say right now."

"But like a relationship or as your assistant or what?" I kept pressing.

"Like I said, I don't know. I understand you don't want to work for me anymore so that's out, especially now that something has already happened between us, but why don't we both go back to New York to figure it out? Stay with me for a while, see what happens." B looked at me with her big blue eyes, knowing I would fold like a deck chair.

My biggest worry at that time was that *B* just wanted me close, not as in a relationship, but as a friend and support, and if I couldn't work for her she would find another way to make it happen. Was she sleeping with me just for me to get back to her? The thought crossed my mind.

Still I said yes.

***

My folks were sad to see us leave, but clever enough to understand there are limits to how long you can live with your parents, especially when you're staying there with your "girlfriend". And by that, I'm not saying *B* was my girlfriend, just that we definitely had something going on outside the friendship zone and I'm pretty sure even my parents picked up on it, no matter how much we tried to stay under the radar.

"You have a funny little smile on your face," *B* told me in the car. She looked happy to be back in the Big Apple.

"Do I? I guess, I'm feeling pretty good right now, I'm getting more and more into the New York style of things."

B smiled, but didn't say anything. She didn't need to.

Her rented apartment was bigger than I remembered it and it felt amazing how time and memory could change space. We could probably have invited the Lakers for basketball practice in the living room if we wanted to. In front of the wall-to-ceiling windows she had placed her easel and on the floor, leaning on the wall with their backs to it, were the paintings she had worked on. I was instantly curious about what was on them, but if she had been keen on showing me, they wouldn't have faced the wall.

She put down her bag, walked over to the tall windows and said, "I really love your parents, Darryl. I know I repeat myself, but you have such a beautiful and relaxed family vibe. But still I couldn't help but miss New York. In fact, I don't know how I could stay in LA for so long." I walked over to her and in a completely spontaneous gesture, I put my arms around her. I felt her tense up at first, but then she relaxed, after all, we were sleeping together almost every night, so it was a natural thing to do. At least to me.

After a while she untangled herself and walked over to the easel. This prompted me to ask, "So what's up with the paintings on the floor? I'm sure they're nice, but I can't see them."

"That's awfully generous of you, because I think they're all shit. Before I left I thought of burning everything. I'm just not cut out to be painting anything, except for possibly a wall."

I walked over there to have a look at her work, but *B* shouted *No!* before I had the chance to. I stopped in the middle of my bent motion and said, "Okay, okay. I won't look. But they're probably ten times better than you think."

"I'm just not ready to let anyone else see them, that's all. They're very personal. And bad." A sad smile surfaced on *B*'s face, she was dead serious about this and she wasn't going to show them to me.

I picked up my luggage in the hallway and asked her where I should put it.

"You can take the bedroom to the left over there," she pointed to the corridor.

I stopped in my tracks, because I had of course hoped to share a bed more permanently by then. Was I already expecting too much? I couldn't shake the thought that maybe the adventure that started so surprisingly in my boyhood room, was ending as abruptly in New York.

But like she was reading my mind, *B* said: "Don't look like a wounded puppy, you'll still get to see me naked - I just don't want to give up any closet space."

Somewhat relieved, I put my bags into the other, smaller, untouched and impeccably furnished bedroom and sat down on the bed. It was far more comfortable than the one back in Clarendon, but I still felt a bit strange, like I wasn't really supposed to be there. And I had nothing to fall back on either if things didn't work out - I was unemployed and pretty much homeless. All I had was *B*. Which was exactly what she wanted.

B shouted to me from the main room, "I told you I fired Julianne, right? I'm sure you must like that piece of news. I'm actually starting to think it's time to get back into the game again, get a new agent who could hopefully land me something different than another predictable love story."

But I kind of like predictable love stories, I thought to myself.

***

B was meeting up with an agent prospect on a recommendation from an actress friend, who said he could develop her career into something even bigger and better, while I was taking a jog through Central Park in an effort to clear my head.

I was nearing my breaking point. I had stayed with *B* for three weeks and although it had been nice, things had not progressed beyond random sexual encounters. In fact, I was starting to feel like some kind of male gigolo - her luxury in-house lover and friend - and I didn't even get paid!

The good thing was, of course, that *B* was both happier and healthier now, seemingly far away from the dark hole she had been in a month before and eager to start working again.

Who was taking care of her scheduling, administration and agent work? Yeah, you guessed it, it was me. I was back in the wheel again, helping her sort her life out during the day and making love to her during the night. And I did this while I was helplessly in love with her and she wasn't with me and that created a sickening feeling of inferiority which kept eating away at me. I hoped Cesar could make some sense out of it, because I'd booked a date with him for the first time in a long time at an organic café, not too many blocks from the Staten Island ferry. Life had changed dramatically for him, he was now in his first serious relationship and put all his energy into that. This was good for him of course, but I missed us staying in touch more frequently.

The Cesar I met at the café was not the Cesar I knew, his hair had grown out and he'd combed it to the side using a can of gel. He was wearing a suit and had a confident, mature air about him, hailing from a good job, a girlfriend and improved looks.

"Wow, look at you!" I said, as we sat down, "that's a promotion alright!"

"You're talking to the head of development," Cesar grinned and that's when I first *really* recognized him, the smile and its goofy, slightly tilted nature, was still there.

"Congratulations. I think *you* owe me lunch today. You know this all started when you cut those nasty locks off."

"I know, I know - they were my bad luck charm. But I've

really tried to turn my life around and I think everything changed when I met Rosa. She just makes me want to push myself and find strengths I didn't even know I had before. It's pretty amazing."

I couldn't imagine the old Cesar ever uttering a line like this, so it was a lot for me to take in.

"Sounds like you're really in love."

Cesar had a dreamy look on his face I'd only seen when he was smoking weed, "Yeah, you could you say that. She's the best thing that ever happened to me."

I took a bite of my muffin and pondered it, "Cesar Livingstone, a soon-to-be married development manager. Never thought I would say something like that."

"Me neither," he said and sipped his cappuccino. "So what's up with you two? Sparks flying, birds twittering?"

"There's a lot of Twitter for sure, but I wouldn't call it sparks. That part is still not happening. We just see things differently, I see a future and to her we're just fuck-buddies until something better comes along."

Cesar looked at me like I just said something remarkably stupid, "It sounds like you're feeling sorry for yourself. Are you sure it can't be that feeling that when you have something really good you're so afraid to lose it, it's almost better not to have it in the first place? It's obvious you're doubting yourself too much and I'm pretty sure she's not very attracted to it either."

I could see Cesar's point, but part of me felt that B very much liked where she had me, in a box, accessible, but without attachments. Problem was, I didn't much like it myself.

"By the way," Cesar said, "what is A thinking about all this? It must be quite a blow to him that you're dating his ex. You were quite close."

"He doesn't know, nobody knows. If you've been working as someone's assistant for a long time you can get away with being seen in public and of course we don't kiss out in the open. I can't really think too hard about his opinion at the moment, he has moved on and to be honest I'm not sure it's something to have an opinion about."

"You sound pretty pessimistic to me and I hate it. What are you doing to yourself, Darryl? You're letting her turn you into someone you're not."

Although his comment angered me at first, Cesar had always had a knack for hitting the nail on the head and here he had managed to do so again, it just hurt too much for me to accept it.

"You have to make it clear to her how you feel and be serious about it too, if she's not interested in anything beyond sex, then I think you should make a stand and move out. It's not dignified to be someone's fuckbuddy, man. Even if she's a superstar."

It sounds so easy when you're sitting on that side of the fence, dude, I thought before I finished my tasteless muffin.

***

I knew I should have listened to Cesar's advice. It was a no-brainer really. But somehow I didn't manage to approach *B* in a good way and my unease was growing progressively, which made me more and more insecure around her. It wasn't what "the relationship" needed, that's for sure, but I was on a slippery slope, mentally sliding into an abyss of lousy confidence. She didn't seem to care too much though, her head was elsewhere: in memorizing movie scripts, upcoming business meetings, her re-energized career. I was happy for her but at the same time sad that our so called "romance" was coming to the inevitable end. I knew it all along of course: a middle class kid from Virginia and a Hollywood movie star - doesn't make much sense does it?

The expense card was back in my hands, but I felt cheap using it, which made sense because it wasn't a job anymore, it was something else. Did it mean she saw me as her assistant again? Possibly. The amount of sex kept decreasing and her spontaneous gestures of affection had completely stopped. I felt used.

Should I've been angry at her for doing this to me? In a way, maybe, but somehow I couldn't. I felt I had been naive enough to put myself in the situation and therefore I had to be mature enough to get out of it. Like it was, we were risking to lose the friendship we had, but I had such a hard time letting go of the rosy moments we had shared together - they lingered in the back of my head like dreams you never wanted to wake up from.

On a personal level, I was stagnating, still with the increasingly vague hope of opening a wine bar, but with no clear path on getting there. I simply didn't have enough energy to think about things like that.

But after my usual morning jog one day, I decided to seize the beautiful weather and pick up lunch and a few books to maybe spark some kind of inspiration. Cesar's girlfriend, the always pleasant Rosa, had recommended a few books which helped her "keep her on her toes". She was a real go-getter: feisty, hyper, not my type, but apparently Cesar's.

I probably looked a bit out of place in the Barnes and

Noble in my shorts and running shirt, but it didn't take me long to locate all the books on Rosa's list. I added a cappuccino and a turkey/cranberry baguette to the shopping list, paid for everything and headed out into Central Park. The sun warmed my face and I felt my spirits lift.

It was exactly what I needed.

I sipped my coffee, ate my under-heated baguette and browsed through the books, read a page here and there and forgot about time completely. I was enjoying myself so much, just letting my sweat dry in the basking sun, that I didn't notice a man sitting down on the bench next to me. He spoke, "Trying to better yourself, huh?"

I looked over at the guy, who had a movie-star face, blindingly white teeth and a one-day stubble. He wore a white Lacoste polo shirt and was holding a large thermos coffee mug. It seemed like he wanted to let me in on a secret.

I was a bit taken aback by this. New Yorkers, as opposed to many other Americans, aren't as keen on starting conversations with strangers and it's perhaps no coincidence that "fuck you" is the most used phrase here. This guy was not the normal grumpy New Yorker, he was supremely confident and relaxed. But, of course, a sweaty dude with running clothes and a stack of self-help books has zero intimidation factor.

"Yeah, I guess. Got some recommendations from a friend."

"Let me see those," he stretched out his hand and expected me to hand him the books. It was kind of forward, but it's not like he was going to steal them, was he? It didn't fit well with his tidy appearance and his shiny golden Rolex watch. Unless he'd stolen that too.

The man scanned the books with his dark brown eyes, "Olson, I've read that. A bit basic, but good. Law of attraction? Controversial stuff, but brilliant marketing. Outselling the Bible for all I know. Aha, Tim Ferriss, somehow I didn't see that one coming. Nice, but slightly weird dude."

He handed the books back to me, "Not a bad idea, reading those. Might take you places. Depending on where you want to go of course." The man took a sip of coffee and looked out over the Great Lawn. For a second he seemed to be lost in thought.

"I felt a bit out of tune so I thought I'd give them a try. You a big fan of this kind of books?" I said, and studied him.

"Not a fan, but I read them. Since I quit my job and got more time, I've started reading a lot more, pretty much anything that comes my way. I like to say that books find me, not the other way around. I also write myself by the way."

"Anything I know?"

Dimples showing clearly in his chiseled face, the guy seemed happy I asked the question, "I don't think you've read them. I've written one on business with a marketing focus and one that's part fiction and part autobiography. It's called The Wake-Up Call. Here's my card."

The card was white with a name and some contact details on it. The name was "Jack Reynolds." and below it it read: "Writer."

I took it and stretched out my hand, "Darryl."

"Nice to meet you, Darryl. You're not a New Yorker are you?"

"Likewise. No, not originally, although I live here now - I'm from Clarendon, Virginia."

"That's a nice area. Myself, I'm a New Yorker through and through, wouldn't live anywhere else."

I got the feeling this guy must have been some kind of top-of-the-line business man, which made me wonder why he was sitting on a park bench in Central Park in the middle of the day, talking to a smelly guy with a pack of books and colorful jogging shoes.

I noticed him looking out over the Great Lawn and followed his eyes to a little girl, not older than a toddler, stumbling around on the grass. Like he knew what I was thinking, he said: "That's my daughter, Amber. She loves coming here."

"Oh, okay. She's cute."

"Thanks, she got her mother's eyes." Jack smiled.

"Can I ask you why you quit working?" I said.

Jack made a grimace, "Oh, that's a helluva long story and I don't have time to get into it right now. But in short, I'll blame and *thank* women for it. They were always central in shaping and changing me. It took me a long time to understand *that* and to be honest with you, I still don't understand *them*."

I couldn't see Jack having any problems *meeting* women though. He was a magnet, testosterone fly-paper.

"It's the same reason I'm on this bench really," I said, modestly, hoping he could give me some advice or at least listen in. I realized I was desperate to talk to anyone willing to listen.

"Don't tell me you're trying to improve yourself because someone else wants you to?"

"I don't think so. I'm doing it for me, but I'm in this weird kind of relationship, it's not even a relationship in that sense actually, where I feel we're slipping away from each other and I really want to reach out to her and stop it - but I'm frozen. I was her assistant for years and now we're lovers, but she's famous and I'm not and I'm struggling big-time with confidence, while she seems to become more independent every day. The fact is that I have really strong feelings for her, but I'm not sure they're mutual." I realized I was sputtering out the words. I was both nervous and in dire need of getting them out.

Jack chuckled, "That's some scenario, might even be a script in it somewhere! I'm not sure I can offer any advice without knowing all the details, but I do know that women hate insecurity and if you have low self-esteem, it's going to drastically decrease your stock value. From the sound of it, I think it's best to just tell her how you're feeling and ask her what she feels about you. Get it out in the open, so you don't run the risk you're worrying about the same things for no good reason."

It was pretty much as I expected - sound advice which was easy to give, but hard to follow.

"A friend of mine said the same thing a while ago, but I just can't seem to get it out of me. Maybe it's because I know what the answer's going to be."

"If you know what the answer's going to be, you don't have much to be afraid of do you? Believe me, you'll feel ten times better afterwards, no matter how it turns out. And if it ends up the way you fear it will, you won't waste any more time worrying and can at least move on with your life."

Jack was right, I was wasting my time living in limbo and it was better to break the whole thing off if it had almost zero chance of survival anyway. I just *had* to deal with it.

"Thanks for the advice. I really appreciate it." I looked down on my stinky clothes, "I'll probably head home for a shower now. But it was nice talking to you."

"Sure, man, anytime. I'm spending an hour in the park almost every day so there's a chance we might run into each other again."

To that I smiled, said bye and left Jack and his daughter.

***

Fast forward a few weeks. I was still living with *B*, but she was on her way to Egypt to scout locations, meet the film crew and talk to the director of an upcoming epic movie, where she had managed to get one of the lead roles. There were no physical interaction between us anymore, but I was still helping her out, being a work-for-free live-in assistant. She'd asked me to come to Egypt with her, but I'd said no. Her new agent, Richard, was going with her so I had the feeling she wasn't going to need me that badly. After all, she hadn't pressed me hard to change my mind. Maybe she was a little bit sick of me.

To compensate for the sadness I felt inside about us, I had decided to put my mind on other things and ask *B* if she wanted to partner with me in business instead. It was such a logical idea, really, but it hadn't hit me in my love-clouded state. Now, when I knew things were not working out between us the way I wanted them to, the idea had come to me almost like in a dream, and I loved it. It would help us stay working together, although living apart, and also be a big step towards achieving my dream. For the situation, it was as much win-win as I could hope for and I desperately wanted her to see it the same way.

You could see it as a friend asking a friend to put wings on his dream.

But I didn't have much time before she flew to Egypt so luckily I had managed to get dinner reservations at a famous Italian restaurant to unleash the plan. Sadly, *B*'s renewed interest in the social life had inspired her to invite a guest, a famous musician that I, again, can't name so let's just call him *J*. They had been hanging out a bit lately, (she had gone to a concert of his and become a fan) and to me it looked just like the start of another one of her doomed love affairs.

It hurt, let me tell you.

But I knew that feeling sorry for myself was the least productive feeling in the world, so I tried to block it, focusing all my energy on my wine bar dream and seeing *B* as the way to make it happen. It was time to move on with my life and find a purpose to occupy my sad and love-stricken mind.

I'd done the ground work already and found a small, two-story, closed-down coffee shop in the Meatpacking district, which I really could envision as an Italian *enoteca*. It needed quite a bit of work, and it would cost me dearly to refurbish the way I wanted it, but that's where *B* came into the picture.

I hoped.

***

Rao's interior never changes - it's the classic of classics. People have been talking about the meatballs and the pasta sauces since it opened, but I'd never gone there and was looking forward to it. *B*, on the other hand, had been there many times as her ex-husband, *A*, loved the place and knew the owner pretty well. I was impressed by the cosy decor, small and homely in a Goodfellas and Godfather kind of way and it being very Italian, I instantly felt at home.

B was wearing a strong-shouldered Balmain dress for the occasion and looked ravishing. I also wanted to dress nicely and had put on my nicest suit (a gift from her), a grey Armani with fine chalk stripes and a crisp light blue shirt. When I looked at myself in the mirror, I had to admit how much she had helped my dress sense, suddenly I knew how to look stylish.

Rao's owner, Frankie (what else?), said "Bella!" and gave *B* a big hug before we were led to our table. Then he told us the menu for the night and I went for the meatballs, while *B* chose a ricotta clamshell pasta. I was studying the wine list while she exchanged a few polite sentences with our table neighbors, a famous business man and his wife.

Sometimes I wondered what they made of me, these powerful and famous people. Did they think, "So who the fuck is this guy?" or were they just assuming I was also famous or just a friend of *B*? Did I have the "assistant look", or could I pull off the illusion of having landed in the spotlight by my own efforts? I got the feeling that most people saw me as an (to them) unknown rapper, which was stereotypical and sad in a way, because I didn't care much for rap music, but it still felt somewhat better than being an assistant.

After choosing a bottle of vintage Valipolicella Ripasso, I asked *B* where her "date" was. It stung a little, asking, but I wanted to get my point across. We had stopped sleeping together, so I had no right to "claim" her in any way, I guess, but it still felt strange how quickly she had "discarded" me.

She gave me an angry look, "It's not a date, we're friends. What's up with you thinking I date everybody? In fact, I just got a text. He's late. He'll join us for dessert or drinks."

B looked disappointed by the news, but I was happy to get her alone for a while. It gave us the chance to talk and properly discuss the things I had on my mind.

After the first sip of wine I saw no point in beating around the bush, but just as I was about to open my mouth she said: "You sure you don't want to come with me to Egypt? It will be fun, we always have such a good time!"

How could you explain you weren't happy being the fifth wheel, when she seemed completely clueless about what was going on? I just *had* to break it to her.

"Sorry, I know it would be fun, but I need to get my own life on track and lately I've felt I'm just floating around like a duck in a pond. What am I to you really? We're not lovers anymore and I'm not your assistant, but I'm still doing an assistant's job. It's already tough being around you when I'm really, really attracted to you and you're not feeling the same about me."

There it was. It was finally out. I think this was the first time I really said how I truly felt, which was kind of ridiculous, but I was working along the lines of *better late than never* and as soon as I had uttered the words, it felt like a weight had been lifted from me.

B looked stung. She hadn't seen it coming and suddenly wore a forlorn look on her face. She looked everywhere but directly at me, then said in a soft voice, "Darryl, I'm still too confused to be in any kind of relationship and you have to understand that. I just got divorced, you've been my assistant for years, it's kind of weird we've been sleeping together, I know, but it's still too soon me for to get involved in anything more serious than that. I don't want to risk our friendship."

Her reply made a lot of sense, but not the kind of sense I wanted.

"*B*, I'm in love with you. I didn't intend for it to happen, after all, we've managed to be around each other for a long time without any emotional drama, but something happened in Rome and it's not easy for me to shut it down. I know it's unfortunate, but I think I need to distance myself a bit from you to be able to go back to being just friends again. Which makes going to Egypt together a stupid idea."

"So I guess we're back to where we were a few months ago? You talking about starting your own life when I really need you." Her mood had suddenly changed a bit, she didn't like this conversation and frankly neither did I. Still, we had to have it.

"But you need me like you need a cuddly animal. It's always at will and when you don't need or want me, you just look the other way. It's very tough for me to be treated like that." I didn't want to bring her down, I just wanted her to understand my side of the story. Apparently, it wasn't that easy.

"Do you think I'm selfish? I'm letting you stay with me, I pay for everything you want, I value you so much and I tell you this as often as I can, and you say I only think of my own good? It's definitely not how I see it! To me we're friends who help each other out."

Things were obviously not going the way I'd hoped, but I'd reached the point of no return: "You're not selfish, I'm just telling you how I *feel*. Things are looking great for you, you have lots of new friends, a new agent, a new movie to make, you don't need me like some old ball-and-chain. I'd love to be your friend, but right now I need some distance. Otherwise I think we'll risk our friendship."

B looked at me with a sour face while I rambled on: "I really need to find my own rhythm and that's all I ask. I move out, but stay in New York and start working on something for myself. Well, actually not only myself," and here I had hoped to launch myself into my proposal in a natural way, because asking for favors was never one of my strong suits, "I have an idea of something we can do together. You know this wine bar I've been talking about? I've seen this place, this great, great location for it. I have everything thought out: budgets, interior, menu, staff, everything. All I need is a little loan to get started."

"A loan?" *B* looked like she had just sunk her teeth into a lemon. It was too late for me to understand that saying I needed distance, but still wanted her money, sounded a bit...lame.

"Yes, not something huge. Just for me to get started. The rest I have saved up. It would really mean a lot to me and you would of course get your money back. You *know* my word is good and all I'm asking for is a small investment. You can either loan me the money or put them in as my partner and we'll own the place together. I promise you we can make it into a success." I tried my best to be convincing and really *sell* the idea, but her reaction made me lose all hope.

"How much money do you need?" *B* struggled to swallow. But like I said, it was all or nothing at this point - so I told her the amount. Which in turn made her look down on her

Prada purse like I was about to snatch it from her.

"I don't think I can do that, Darryl. Not that I wouldn't want to, but it's quite a bit of money and my finances hasn't exactly been growing these last few months without work. I'm also paying quite a steep rent. I really needed to take on another film project to get some more cash flow. I'm sorry - I know this is your dream and all, but right now isn't the time."

In retrospect, I should've seen this coming but at the time it was still a mighty punch in the gut. I told her I understood, because I knew there wasn't any point in pressing further. When it came to these types of decisions, *B* was exactly like Barry - she wouldn't change her mind.

The rest of the evening I was left with a fake smile on my lips and a sinking feeling in my stomach. *J* arrived like promised, for the dessert. He was dressed in a v-necked white t-shirt, a cheap-looking silver chain Jesus and a grey blazer with his sleeves rolled up like Miami Vice. His faded jeans were hanging from his skinny butt and his arms were loaded with tattoos. *B* was obviously quite taken by him and he seemed to be too. Taken by himself that is.

I don't know how I managed to keep calm and take it, but I did. I saw them exchange jokes and smiles and look so goddamn worry-free that for a second I felt like throwing my wine glass in their faces and leave. *Take that you rich and soulless motherfuckers! How does the wine taste when you got it through your nose?*

After dinner, which I barely enjoyed despite it probably being my life's only opportunity to eat at Rao's, the two lovebirds wanted to hit the club while I wanted to hit a wall. With my head.

Instead I went home. Although *B*'s apartment wasn't

exactly home anymore.

***

The next two days I spent most of my time walking around with a sullen look on my face and my hands in my pockets. *B* was leaving for Egypt and I was left alone in her apartment, without anything but my cracked heart to mend. The only good thing was that I didn't need to be around her anymore - it had become close to unbearable. I still loved her, but I'd completely given up on the idea of us together and every time I saw her I was reminded of that. She probably felt it too, my disappointment in not "having" her, and as an added "bonus" my disappointment about her not helping me. I had expected too much and I scolded myself for it.

The hug before she left to the airport was painful and I struggled to hold back my tears.

"Thanks for looking out for the apartment for me." She said with her face close to my ear.

"No worries," I said, fighting a strong impulse to smell her hair. Oh, how I loved her hair. And her smell.

She removed herself from my arms, "Just know that the offer of being my assistant is still up for grabs." And then she blew me a kiss, took her Louis Vuitton travel kit and walked out of the apartment and inside the elevator.

This left me without a plan, in an apartment which wasn't mine, with a credit card which wasn't mine, in a life which couldn't be mine.

Needless to say, I wasn't feeling great.

I took a long shower where I almost broke down in tears - and I never cry. I had no idea how to move on in my *B*-less existence and I couldn't stop mentally punishing me for being naive enough to fall for her...again. I'd probably never felt more lonely in my life than those hours after she left me. I didn't want to disturb Cesar, who had more or less faded away from my life and was spending 99 percent of his time with Rosa. I couldn't move back to Clarendon again, because I couldn't take the feeling of defeat. I had to do something, something unexpected. I had to take a risk.

And that's where I made up my mind to take most of my savings, get a loan, put the deposit on the dusty old coffee shop and move in there. I had to take things as they came and if that meant doing the place up myself using whatever materials and furniture I could afford, that would be it. I had to go out in the world and be my own man, no matter how uncomfortable it was compared to the life I was in. I took the cherished expense card from my wallet and put it on *B*'s nightstand.

The dream ride was over. And in some little way it felt good.

***

I coughed dust for days cleaning the place up. I watched my bank account rapidly disintegrate. I spent sleepless nights in the tiny loft, thinking what the hell I was doing. But things progressed, slowly, slowly, my humble *enoteca* taking shape.

It wasn't only *my* own blood, sweat and tears that was spilled, because my father blessed me by bringing his expertise, building materials from his company, and also some money in helping me getting the place ready. I still didn't have enough to make it exactly how I wanted, but at least I was doing my best.

B texted me twice from Egypt, she seemed in a joyous mood, but wrote that she missed me. I replied that I was busy working on getting my wine bar ready and that things were progressing, albeit at a slow pace. Then the communication ceased. Maybe because I wanted it too. The only way I could get over was to let her fade out and not be in the forefront of my brain all the time. She probably understood this, and let me be and heal.

And I slowly did. I locked all my energy into my business and although it was becoming somewhat of a "compromise", I was thrilled to finally be doing something for me and me only. I was living in a sparse and microscopic loft with a rusty bathtub in the kitchen and a cooking plate to boil noodles from - quite a contrast from the glamorous existence in the Johnson mansion - but still I felt better than I had in a long time. Cesar had been right, it was about time I got my chunky ass out from my padded life and into reality.

My father was helping me choose lounge chairs when I got the text. I was frustrated because everything was so expensive. I had always liked the vintage leather style, but everything I really wanted would take a big bite from my budget. I pulled up my cracked iPhone from my back pocket and opened the message. It was from *B* and it said, "Made a small contribution to your project. It's in your bank account. And it's a gift, not a loan :) Good luck. Love x."

After reading it, it was like someone had let loose an animal inside of me and I could hardly sit still. I had to get some air.

I told my father the news and suggested we have lunch so I could check the bank account and ponder how much this changed things. The amount was of essence of course, although any sum would have been appreciated.

I went to the nearest ATM and what my bank statement told me made me jump up in the air and shout. Suddenly I had the financial freedom to make my vision come alive. All thanks to *B*.

It was impossible not to love that girl.

My father and I toasted to my good fortune. I wore a silly smile on my face and said, "I just can't believe it. I never thought she would do something like this."

"Why not? She cares for you, it's obvious. And she has the money."

"Yeah, but she told me she had to be careful. But maybe her circumstances has changed now, with her latest role and everything. Or maybe she just sees things differently."

"She has maybe realized how good you are for her. She probably wants you back." My father tried.

"Hold your horses dad, I'm sure it's not that. I'd rather think she's feeling guilty for how she used me and wants to pay me back. But I'm okay with that, it's not a bad compensation."

In all honesty, if someone asked me if I wanted a big sack of money to fulfill my dream or for *B* and I to be together ever after, I would obviously choose the latter. But if I couldn't have that, a sack of money was pretty good.

I texted her after lunch: "You're the BEST! I'll pay you back every cent, I promise. THANKS SO MUCH. xxx." (Capital letters are okay when you feel as ecstatic as I did).

After that things got easier. I picked the furniture and the finishings I wanted. I could invest in a good selection of wines. I would make my desired launch date. Everything was coming together.

The weeks passed incredibly fast. I got into a flow and things started happening consistently to my advantage. My parents even came to New York for two weeks to help me get set up properly.

It's good I didn't know how much hard work setting up a wine bar would involve, because chances are I wouldn't have gone through with it. But I've learned that sometimes it's good just to fumble ahead in life and not worry too much about the consequences. I, the non-risk-taker, was suddenly risking something and it was exactly what I had to do.

I became a multi-talent. Or at least a multi-doer. I painted, bought supplies, interviewed for staff, bought cutlery, furniture and sweated buckets while doing so. The whole thing was so much work, I ended up shedding weight, looking healthier than I've done since I was 12 and had my first real love affair with the cheeseburger.

In the end, not only I did I look better than I had before, but the enoteca surpassed my expectations. The relaxed lounge style was there, the cigar room feel, the soft lighting, the plush velvet chairs, the bar with countless of expensive wine bottles on the wall, even my little attic was kind of cozy now - after all, I'd spent basically all my time there and would be for quite a while more. At least until I had enough money to rent or buy a proper apartment. I'd really put my heart and soul into this project and I was dying to see if it would pay off.

Cesar and Rosa actually helped me a lot with the marketing, spreading the word, putting up flyers, getting a guy from Cesar's work to set up a professional website. Everything and everyone came together just beautifully and my dream was coming true at last.

The only thing that concerned me was that I hadn't

heard from *B* since her deposit into my account.

***

On opening night I was a bundle of nerves. Months of work were falling into place and my ego couldn't take anything but a roaring success. Failure would kill me. Almost literally. Luckily, I had my friends and parents there with me, Cesar and Rosa at one table, my parents Lynne and Robert at another, giving their support and also making the place look less empty. I had my fresh staff of four: chef Lorenzo, bartender Matt, and waitresses Rachel and Deena, and of course myself, doing a little bit of everything. I had managed to set up a little stage in the corner, where a young local jazz trio, also from the university (thanks Matt!) were playing standards with great passion. Thankfully all the publicity, marketing and word-of-mouth had helped - the place was soon buzzing with wine, platters, music and talk, while I was running around like crazy, making sure everyone was enjoying themselves. Which they seemed to be.

The idea as such was simple and since we didn't offer any real dishes besides different varieties of platters, we weren't stretched beyond what we could handle. This was why I wanted to open a wine bar and not a restaurant, because its all about the wine, the atmosphere and the company - not so much the food. And that has saved me from a lot of additional headache.

I poured a glass for my father and he looked up under his big, bushy eyebrows with a smile on his face, "I can't believe this is really happening! It's a huge success, son. I'm so proud of you."

"Let's not get ahead of ourselves, dad. It's a fantastic first night, I agree, but without your help it couldn't have happened." And without *B*'s financial push, of course.

"Yeah, we helped, but this place is all you, your dream, your hard work, *you*. And it makes me so damn happy to see it come to life! And the wine," he added almost as an afterthought, "is of course spectacular." He raised his glass towards me and took a full sip.

I nodded my head as to say, *I know, I know* and rushed off to another table to take their order and then to Cesar and Rosa to check on how they were doing. The couple was laughing and talking as usual, lucky to be so in-tune. I still had a hard time believing Cesar's good luck.

"It's brilliant, man," Cesar said, and gave me a slap on the back. "Congratulations, Darryl!" Rosa added, and put her slender arms around me in a hug. I was a lucky man to have friends like them to share my big moment. Their excitement on my behalf was genuine and it warmed my heart.

"It's a bit early to tell, but right now it's looking pretty good," I said and smiled.

"Sure as hell it does. And the band is on fire." Cesar sent thumbs up to the guys playing in the corner. They sure did their part in making the place more energetic and alive. And for the first month, I didn't even have to pay them - it was a test to see if it would work and they were happy to be playing for a live audience.

The only regret I had on this glorious and satisfying night was that *B* wasn't a part of it.

***

At almost two in the morning I was alone, cleaning up the last bits from the opening night. The staff, my parents, the band, my friends, everyone had gone home, all excited about the turnout but obviously exhausted too. I was dead tired myself, but too excited to get a proper night's sleep straight away. I needed to let my head wind down properly, have a glass of wine and let the whole thing sink in.

When I had finished cleaning, I went over to the bar and poured myself a glass of the Antinori I had gotten through one of Jorge's wine contacts and prepared myself a small platter with *parmeggiano*, brie, parma ham, honey, olives and ciabatta bread. Then I sat down in one of the leather chairs and took a deep breath. I was too tired to read so I just sat there, drained of energy, breathing slowly and thinking about the day that had passed by so quickly it was impossible to piece it all together.

But the wave of relief didn't last longer than ten minutes, because someone knocked on the door. I was worried at first that it would mean trouble, but luckily I had the CCTV cam to rely on. And what it showed me sent a jolt through my body. I shivered to the image of *B*, standing outside my door, looking severely uncomfortable. Shocked, I went over there to open.

"Hi Darryl." She didn't look well, in fact it looked like she had been crying.

"Come in," I said, and closed the door after her. She walked over to a chair and slumped down in it.

"Wine?" I said like I had talked to her yesterday.

"Yes, please."

I went over to the kitchen and poured her a glass, but couldn't avoid spilling a bit because my hands were shaking so badly.

I sat in the chair opposite and pushed the tray I'd prepared over to her, "There's more if you want."

"I'm okay," she said, but she didn't look it one bit.

"Wow," she said after a little while, "the place really looks fantastic. I'm so happy for you."

But she didn't look happy that's for sure.

"How are you?" I said.

But *B* didn't reply, instead she started crying.

I didn't know what to do so I walked over to her, kneeled down by her side and hugged her. I hugged her as hard as I could and she hugged me back. I felt tears well up inside, tears of exhaustion, tears of blocked-out emotions, tears from seeing my best friend in pain.

"I don't know, Darryl," she said, when the tears had stopped flowing, "I don't know what to do with myself."

"What do you mean?" I said, as softly as I could.

"I'm happy, then I'm miserable, I'm happy, then I'm miserable. I have no middle ground. I don't know how to feel *normal*."

At that point I wanted to kiss her and reassure her that everything was going to be okay. But it would be the wrong thing to do, so I didn't.

"What's wrong? Did something happen at the film shoot or what?"

"No, everything is good. Should be good. And that's the problem - everything's fine but I feel like the loneliest and most miserable person in the world. I know I'm not, of course I know, but I can't maintain that feeling without sinking into a black hole and I'm so tired of being down there. *It sucks!*"

We shared a sad smile to that. *B* had a way of sprinkling humor into the most dire circumstances. It was a style of communication we shared - you could even say it was our own private little way of talking.

"You're lonely," I said.

"Yes, I'm horribly lonely."

"Why didn't you call me before?"

B took a napkin and dabbed her eyes, "I just couldn't do it to you. I don't *want* to be here. It's not right. You're in love with me and I just *need* you, I can't play around with your feelings anymore."

Something sank inside of me. For a second I hated her, I absolutely hated her. Why couldn't she just love me? She NEEDED me, she wanted me by her side, why was *loving* me so fucking difficult?

"Okay," I said, not sure how to proceed, was this what she was so miserable about?

"I'm sorry, Darryl, I really am."

"You're sorry, I'm sorry, I guess we're both sorry about the situation," I said coldly and rose from my knees. I didn't want her and her self-pity in my bar anymore, I wanted to be alone.

"Don't be angry with me. I can't take it when you're angry with me!"

I sipped my glass of wine and looked at her. And suddenly I saw a five-year-old girl in front of me instead of the woman I was in love with.

"What do you want me to do then?"

"I want you to be my friend. I hope we can go back to what we had that felt so good."

"So the money you gave to me, they had some kind of condition that I had to come back as your assistant?"

"No, they are a gift. They're yours no matter if we never see each other again. Don't talk stupid."

My anger was slowly dissipating, but instead I felt helplessness. Could I let *B* back into my life again? Or was it love or nothing?

After a while I found my voice, "Why did you come this late and not for the opening? I could've been asleep by now."

B looked down, "I wasn't planning to see you, but then I couldn't sleep and it got so bad I suffered something like a panic attack and I couldn't stand to be alone. I'm terrified, Darryl. I don't know what's wrong with me, why I can't just relax and enjoy my life."

"Maybe you should take another break? Call off your engagements?"

"It's not about work, at least I'm not lonely there, but I don't want to live only when I work. That's exactly the kind of person I *don't* want to be."

"Okay," I said. I didn't know where the conversation was leading. She was lonely and panicking again, I was happy about my success, but still heartbroken. Something had to give.

"I have a proposal for you. If you agree to see a therapist to deal with the demons in your brain, I'll move in with you again." My mouth said, but I wasn't sure if my brain was involved. Moving back with *B* could potentially be very, very painful to me.

"Could you? I mean, I don't want you to be my assistant or lover, I just want you to be my friend."

I was losing the battle I had promised myself not to lose, but at this point I was too tired to care. Maybe things looked different after a night's sleep.

"I can't promise you it will be easy, it might not work out at all," I said to buy myself the chance of changing my mind.

B suddenly looked relieved, like a huge knot had been untied inside of her. She looked at me and said, "You were really in love with me weren't you? Why didn't you show it more then? Most of the time after Clarendon you were stale and uncomfortable, it was like too different people."

I couldn't really disagree with her, I had been too self-conscious and lacked the confidence to be in a relationship with her. It must have showed more than I thought.

"I was intimidated and confused by the situation. What could I really offer you? A few jokes? A shoulder to cry on? That's not really enough for a relationship, no matter how much I wanted it to be."

B's voice went up a pitch when I said this, "I'm sorry but what the fuck are you talking about? You're the nicest guy I've ever met and you really bring out the best in me. Why do you think I want you around all the time? To think you have no chance to be in a relationship with me is all in your head, no-one else's. And that's perhaps the problem."

This fueled me on. "Come on now! That's what all girls say, *you're too good for me.* It's just bullshit to make themselves feel more okay about hurting someone."

B collected herself and took a long sip from her glass, "The point I want to make, Darryl, is that I need you in my life. I don't really know in which form yet, but I guess that will show. Only that I need you. That's all I can say right now."

Her words made me uneasy. Was there a chance for *us* somewhere down the road? A chance I had completely discarded before she showed up on my doorstep and stirred things up again. I knew somewhere that right now wasn't the time, that the best thing would probably be to say no, stay away from each other and not get confused again. I needed to put all my energy into my business and had neither time nor energy for heartbreak.

Part of me wanted to say no for exactly that reason, not to affect the positive path I was on, the good feeling and the *flow* I was experiencing at the moment, and a small part of me also wanted to say no to hurt her, to revenge how she hurt me, and to show her she doesn't always get what she wants.

But then again, it was *B*. The person I'd recently found out I loved more than I had ever loved anyone. And if there was a chance with her, even if it was the tiniest, shitty little iota of a chance, then I better take it.

So I took it.

***

Epilogue

I know you might want the happy ending, the one where *B* and I fell in love and lived happily together ever after, but sadly, that's not how life works. This doesn't mean the ending or whatever end we're coming towards isn't happy, because we're both happy being friends as I write this. It just didn't work out towards a relationship, and no matter how heartbreaking this might sound, it's all for the best.

We're both still single, although dating other people at the time of writing. I'm happy to say I've been able to let go and settle for a friendship where we can help each other towards something better without confusing things. Despite how spectacular I felt at times during the brief fling I've described in this book, I've also realized that I was somewhat blinded by the circumstance, being able to capture the heart of a sought-after world class celebrity.

It was a major rush that twisted and turned my head and heart from being madly in love to being deeply depressed.

In a way I'm very lucky it happened, because it brought me out of my slightly anti-social, workaholic shell and made me understand a lot about love, friendship and, perhaps most of all, myself. It has helped me grow as a person and forged an even stronger bond between B and I.

It has made me realize that I'm a lucky man.

Another reason I'm lucky man, is that my wine bar has become a popular hangout. It's actually become so popular that I'm playing around with the idea of opening a restaurant in the same style together with Jorge. It's a long-term project, but it would be exciting to work together again and I know no better chef than my good friend.

Talking about Jorge, last night B and I went to his son's release party. Luís talent and hard work has finally paid off and his music can now be heard on MTV, in radio and purchased in stores and on iTunes. I'm really happy for him and his father and proud that I was gutsy enough to believe in him. Who knows what lies in his path, but it's a great satisfaction to feel that no matter how little experience I have in the music industry, my gut feeling was right - the guy's really good. Screw you, Barry Waldruff, because Luís is going places.

B has also gone places since she came to the enoteca and opened her heart. She has started seeing a therapist and made an effort to bridge the gap between her and her mother. So far it's gone really well, and the woman I meet every week for lunch is far from the train-wreck who laid her innards out on the red carpet. Her eyes are so much happier now and she tells me she limits herself to a few glasses of wine per week. I can't tell you how happy I am that my friend is doing well.

I've realized through telling this story and thinking about what *B* and I've been through in our relationship, that true friendship is one of the most beautiful things in life and it would be a shame not to treat it with utmost care and love.

Be there for one another. It's as simple as that.

In saying so, I know our friendship wasn't always the easiest one. We've had plenty of ups and downs and have gone from working together, to friends, to lovers and back to friends again. It's been a crazy ride, but in the end we've always come back to the understanding that we need each other.

So let's raise our glasses and toast to friendship that goes beyond what's expected and remains through the harshest of storms. After all, this is the substance of life and relationships in its most core element, and that alone is worthy of celebration.

Cheers.

/Darryl

THE END.

ABOUT THE AUTHOR

Jonas is currently the creative director of one of the most successful online gaming groups in the world. He has previously worked as an advertising consultant, copywriter and a journalist. When he's not working he cherishes each moment with his family Lenah and Aiden and whatever time there is left, he spends writing, reading and playing tennis. He's passionate about traveling and wine and thinks New York is the greatest city in the world. He lives with his family on the Mediterranean island of Malta.